FLUKE

FLUKE
James Herbert

NEW ENGLISH LIBRARY

To Kerry and Emma

First published in Great Britain by New English Library, 1977
Copyright © by James Herbert, 1977
All rights reserved. No part of this publication may be
reproduced or transmitted, in any form or by any means,
without permission of the publishers.

First NEL paperback edition June 1978
Reprinted July 1979
Reprinted February 1980
Reprinted November 1980
Reprinted June 1981
Reprinted July 1981
Reprinted October 1981
Reprinted January 1982
Reprinted March 1983

NEL Books are published by
New English Library,
Mill Road, Dunton Green,
Sevenoaks, Kent.
Editorial office: 47 Bedford Square,
London WC1B 3DP

Made and printed in Great Britain by
Hunt Barnard Printing Ltd,
Aylesbury, Bucks.

0 450 05325 3

PART ONE

One

The warmth from the sun beat against my eyelids, soft persuasion to open them. Noises crept into my ears then burst through to my consciousness, confusing sounds, a gabble broken by strident pitches.

Cautiously, almost unwillingly, I half opened my eyes, the sleep in them sticky, a soft moist glue. Through the blur I saw a dark furry body, big as me. It heaved rhythmically up and down, up and down, in a contented sleep. My mouth opened wide as a yawn escaped and my eyes suddenly snapped fully open. Other bodies lay around me, blacks and greys – mixtures of both – some of the coats short and straight, others tufty and curly. A flash of white leapt over me and I felt sharp teeth nip at my ear. I pulled away with a whimper. Where was I? Who was I? *What* was I?

Smells came to my nostrils, unpleasant at first and then strangely pleasing. I wrinkled my nose, breathing in the fumes, powerful odours that somehow made me secure. I wriggled my body closer to the other warm bodies, away from the energetic white pest that finally gave up and bounded towards the surrounding wire. He stood up on his hind legs, resting his paws on the top of the wiring, his rump and stubby tail waggling excitedly. A huge pallid hand reached down and he was lifted away out of sight.

I whimpered again, this time with shock. The hand – so big, so strong! And the smells emanating from it – so alien. Frightening, yet . . . interesting. I tried to snuggle further into the packed lumps of sluggish fur, seeking a contact I didn't understand. Why was I surrounded by these monster animals and why did I feel so akin to them?

The sleep had left me now and my body quivered with awareness. I was in some sort of pen – it looked very large to me – the floor of which was covered in straw. The wiring around us was high, much higher than me, and my companions were dogs. I don't think I really felt fear at that moment; probably just confusion. I remember my breath coming out in short panting gasps and I think I urinated a little, just a trickle. I know I tried to burrow even further between two plump bodies, with two of which I felt some association, some common bond. Now I can guess it was because we were related, but at the time I reacted to instinct alone.

I peeped around me, keeping my head low, my jaw firmly tucked into the straw. Everything was so muted, the colours barely distinguishable apart from their varying tones, only hues of greys and muddy browns. Yet I saw the colours in my mind's eye because I had known them before . . . before . . .

Before?

In my bewildered state even the question, let alone the answer, evaded me.

But now colours were already beginning to filter through, a legacy left to me, a gift that separated me from my fellow creatures. The soft greys turned to light browns, the denser greys to darker browns. The blacks remained black, but deeper. The rainbows flew at me, filling my head with a dazzling variegation, blinding in its intensity. The blacks were no longer black, but blue, indigo, hundreds of shades of browns. The colours hurt my eyes and I was forced to close them. Yet the sun still stung through and the colours still exploded before me. And then the spectrum took its proper order, the colours found their correct balance; the flashes became subdued, the tones began to relate to each other. I opened my eyes and the brief monochrome world had vanished and been replaced by a rich, moving canvas where each colour belonged to itself yet interlocked and shared with its opposites. Even today, I still delight in everything I see, new, surprising colours revealing themselves without warning, seeming to be borne freshly before me only for me to realise they'd always been there but that I'd never really looked. The colours are more muted now, but still fresher and more interesting that they'd been in the past. I suppose it's something to do with the world being bigger to me; being closer to the ground somehow makes me closer to nature.

Having passed through this curious stage I neither understood nor appreciated, I began to be a little more adventurous in my exploration. I lifted my head from the straw and stretched my neck upwards. Faces passed by, looking down at me, funny tender smiles on them. At that time, they all looked the same to me; I couldn't tell male and female apart, nor one individual from another. Nor did I know what they were exactly. Strangely enough, I could tell the difference between the smaller giants right from the start, not just from the elders, but as individuals. Several looked down at me, laughing and making strange noises with their mouths, peering expectantly at the taller ones behind. Above these giants I could see enormous grey-brick buildings stretching far into the sky – and the sky itself seemed so blue, so deep and so clear. Sky is the purest thing I've ever known, whether it's the cold azure of dawn, the striking cobalt of day, or the deepest silver-perforated blackness of night. On the darkest day, when the sky is masked by sullen clouds, the tiniest patch of blue makes my heart jump a little. It seemed then as if I were seeing sky for the first time, and in a way I was – through different eyes.

I gazed rapturously at the blue ceiling for several moments until the rays of the sun made my eyes mist over, causing me to blink rapidly. It was then I realised what I was. I wasn't shocked, for my new brain was still functioning mainly as it should and memories were still lying dormant within it. I accepted what I was; only later did I question my new beginning. But at that time, I thought it was perfectly normal to be a dog.

Two

Is it doubt I sense in you, or something more? Maybe a little fear. All I ask is that you let your mind listen, that you forget for a moment your prejudices and beliefs; when I've finished my story you can decide for yourself. There's a lot that's not clear to me yet and I know it never will be – not in this existence anyway – but I may help you to understand your life a little more. And I may help you to be less afraid.

As I looked around, my vision so different to yours, I felt the fur at the back of my neck being tugged, and suddenly the straw bed dropped away leaving my paws waggling frantically in empty air. A huge rough hand came up from beneath and the pressure was taken off the taut skin at my neck as my bottom was given support. I didn't like the smell of the hands at all, or their hardness. Each smell was separate and mostly new to me. They didn't blend together to make one complete odour; each had its own identity and combined to represent the man. It's difficult for me to explain, but as humans identify each other by assembling in their mind's eye the various features of another person – the shape of the nose, the colour of the eyes, hair, general skin tones, the set of the lips, the build of the body – we animals find it easier to assemble through our senses the various body smells. They're much more reliable, for physical features can be disguised or may change through age, but there's no disguising your own personal scent. It's a gradual build-up from everything you've done in your time and no amount of scrubbing can erase it. The food you've eaten, the clothes you've worn, the places you've visited; that's what gives us your identity, and no visual aspect is more recognisable.

I suppose the giant (I still had no concept of man at that point) who lifted me from the pen reeked of tobacco, booze, fatty foods and the aroma I've found is ever present – sex – but at the time they were all new to me and, as I've said before, frightening, unpleasant, yet interesting. The only familiar smell was the doggy one, and my sensitive nose sought this out and clung to it for comfort. I could now see what seemed like millions and millions of two-legged animals shuffling backwards and forwards, their noises hurting my ears and baffling me. I was in a street-market, of course, and even in those early stages there was some recognition, some familiarity with the place. Rough, growling sounds came from somewhere close to my ear and I snapped my head round nervously. The lips of the creature that held me were moving and these were the source of the growling noises. I don't say I recognised the actual words then, but I understood the intent.

Another voice spoke on the other side of me and I was thrust forward into another pair of arms. The aroma was so different. I suppose the food and drink smells were still there, but the nicotine stench was absent. And there was so much more. You can smell kindness; it's like a fragrance. It's not that interesting, but it's reassuring. There wasn't too much of it, but compared to the hands I had just left, it was like suddenly being sprayed by the finest perfume. I began to lick the hands, for there were still traces of food on them. It's such a treat to lick a human hand or face; the sweat on every part of a human body still holds the food recently eaten and the saltiness gives it a special tang of its own. The taste is subtle and soon gone, but the delicate flavour, combined with the ticklish scratching of tongue against skin, is an exquisite pleasure every dog loves. It's not affection, you see (although after a while a familiar taste is more pleasurable than a strange one and almost becomes a show of love) but more an exercise for appreciative taste-buds.

While one hand hugged me against the friendly giant's chest, the other stroked my head and softly tickled me behind the ears. This sent me into raptures and I tried to nip his nose. He jerked his head away with a sound I could only interpret as a happy growl so I increased my efforts to reach that bulbous feature on

11

his face. My tongue touched his chin and scratched against its roughness. This surprised me a little and I drew back, but the excitement overcame me again and I launched myself forward in a fresh attack. This time, firm hands restrained me.

The voices bartered to and fro and suddenly I was placed back in the pan. I immediately jumped up again, trying to reach the friendly giant, my front paws resting on the wooden top of the wiring. A white body joined me and attempted to shoulder me out of the way. I pushed back though, realising something nice might be about to happen to me and I saw several pieces of greenish paper pass over my head to the rough red hands of my keeper. Then I was in the air again, hoisted high and hugged to the kind-smelling giant-creature's chest. I let out a little yelp of glee and tried to lick the huge face above me. I don't know if or what I suffered under the care of the other giant, but something told me it was good to get away from him; badness poured from his body. Looking down at the other bundles lying there, I felt a pang of regret; they were my brothers, my friends. Sadness swept through me as I was carried away and a vision of a much bigger dog, probably my mother, flashed into my head. I wept then and cowered into the huge creature. At the sound of my whimpers his hand began to stroke my body and soft tones came from his lips.

The crowds of two-legs were even more frightening now I was moving among them and I began to shiver with fear. Everything, everyone, was so big. I tried to snuggle my head inside a fold of the big animal's skin and he allowed me, sympathising with my fright, quietly reassuring me. Now and again I would peep out, but the noise, the flashing colours, the bustle, would soon send my head digging back deeper inside the loose skin, the beat from the broad chest having a strange calming effect on me. Soon we had left the market-place and a new, more terrifying sound roared in my ears.

My head jerked out from its hiding place and my jaw dropped open with fresh terror at the sight of the huge monsters bearing down on us, then whisking by in a whirlwind of disturbed air, seeming to miss us only by inches. They were strange animals to me, much stranger than the animal that carried me, and fearsomely devoid of any character except power and size. Their fumes were nauseating and lacked any food or sweat smells. A worse monster was to appear: brilliantly red and four times the size of the other creatures. I just had time to notice its legs were round and whirled at a tremendous rate before I leapt from my bearer's arms, spilling droplets of urine on to the grey concrete as I dashed away from the approaching beast. Shouting noises sounded from behind me, but my legs refused to stop running as I dodged between the giants who tried to block my path. A foot stretched out in front of me, but I flew over it without even breaking my stride. I veered off course as big hands reached down to grab me, leaving the pavement, throwing myself into the river of fast-moving monsters. Screeches filled my head and dark shapes loomed over me, but I kept running, my eyes focused only on what lay ahead, the advantage of my new-found wide periphery not used, my whole being concentrated on a dark hole that lay ahead of me. And then a memory stirred: *I was something else for a moment, high off the ground, and the fear inside me then was the same as the fear inside me now. Something hurled itself at me, something white and blinding. Then the light exploded into pain*, and I was a dog again, fleeing in a straight line across the paths of screeching cars and buses.

It must have been then that things were triggered off inside me: memories, feelings, instincts – I don't know what – flickered, were aroused, but were not yet exposed, uncovered. They had been woken and had begun to live, but my canine brain was not yet ready to receive them.

I entered the shop doorway I'd been heading for and skidded along the floor in an effort to prevent myself crashing into a tall thing which held brightly coloured squarish objects. It tottered dangerously as my scurrying body struck and hands clutched at it while voices were raised in alarm. I found another hole to scoot into and whipped through it, round a corner and into a nice secure dark area. I cowered there, shivering, my jaw open and my tongue hanging down like a long streak of loose liver. My stomach heaved as I drew in short, sharp panting breaths. My sanctuary didn't last long though: hands grabbed me by the scruff of the neck and rudely tugged me from the recess. Angry growls flayed at me and I was pulled along the floor, my yelps of protest ignored. My head was cuffed several times, but I don't think I felt any pain. I reached the bright doorway and tried to dig my paws into the unhelpful shiny floor. I had no desire to be back out there among those murderous creatures.

A dark shape appeared in the doorway and familiar smells came to my nostrils. I still wasn't sure of the giant but instinct told me he was all I had. He came forward and I allowed him to lift me without protest. I sought out the steadying beat of his heart again and tried to shut out the angry sounds around me. The thumping from inside his chest had a different rhythm now, slightly faster, but I still derived great comfort from it. Tempers, if not actually soothed, were checked, and I found myself out in the open again, this time held more firmly, fingers digging into my soft body like iron rods. Fresh sweat glands had been aroused in my protector and new smells released; I was soon to learn that these were the smells of anger or distress. He carried me along the road, his voice scolding and misery dragged at my spirits.

Gradually, his heartbeat slowed to a more comforting pace and his grip lost its rigidity. A hand found the back of my ear again and began to stroke it, eventually calming my shaking body. Soon I had plucked up the courage to withdraw my nose from inside his jacket and look up at him. As he brought his head down I licked his nose and once again sniffed the smells of affection. His face changed in a strange way, and that was when I first began to recognise expressions and associate them with feelings. It was the start for me, the thing that set me apart from others of my kind. Maybe it *was* the shock of the roaring traffic that in some way had set off remembrances in me, shocked my system into a freakish awareness; or perhaps it would have happened in its own time anyway. At the time, though, I knew the big creatures that moved so fast on round legs were something to be feared – and for me, to be despised.

The man suddenly broke his stride and turned to his left, pushing open a heavy piece of wood and stepping through. The stale atmosphere engulfed me; the contrast between the bright sunshine outside and this cool, dim, smoke-filled cavern

14

was awesome. The hubbub of sound was confined within walls and rebounded from them; the smells, the foul smoke, were contained and magnified, and, overriding all, came a powerful smell which filled every nook and cranny, pungent and bitter.

The man moved forward and set me down between his foot and a gigantic wooden wall, a wall he was able to lean over so that half his body disappeared from view. I peered round his legs and studied the other animals standing about the place in groups, their commotion making a rich, interesting sound, unlike the sharper, less friendly, noises of the market. Everyone seemed to be holding clear bowls of liquid in their hands which they raised to their lips and poured into their mouths. It was fascinating. I saw others sitting around the walls with the various-coloured liquids set on a sort of platform before them. Again, something familiar stirred within me but I wasn't yet ready to pursue the thoughts.

Something wet struck my head and instinctively I flinched. Several huge pats of liquid splattered on the floor before me and I backed away against the wall. I couldn't go far, for I was surrounded by legs, rearing up like thick tree-trunks around me. But curiosity soon overcame my wariness of the wet, shiny pools. My nose twitched and I inched forward, the smell from the liquid not as unpleasant as it had originally seemed. I bobbed my nose over one pool then moved on to another. Rashly I stuck my tongue into it and lapped up the liquid. The taste was ghastly but it made me realise how thirsty I was. I quickly moved to the other puddles and licked them dry. It took about three seconds, I think, to clear that small area of drips. I gazed expectantly up at the man, but he was ignoring me, his body hunched over, head out of vision. I could hear the familiar sounds he made over the general din. I shied away as a strange hand reached down for me and patted my head. I sniffed and the smells were good; I sensed friendliness.

A roundish, yellow-brown object was shoved under my nose and against my mouth. The saltiness reached my taste-buds and released waters in them. Without further thought, I snapped at the proffered food and crunched it into gooey mash. It was crisp yet oily, full of lovely flavours; it was delicious. I swallowed three in quick succession and shuffled my hindquarters in anticipation of more, my head craning upwards, jaws half open. No more was offered me, and as the figure moved away a funny gurgling noise came from his throat. Disappointed, I studied the ground for any small crumbs that may have escaped my munching teeth. Soon, the floor around me became a very clean area. I gave a little yap at the man above me, demanding his attention. But still he ignored me, and I became a little cross. I pulled at the soft skin that hung over his hard feet (it was a little time before I realised these tall creatures wore other animal's skins and in fact *couldn't* shed their skin at will).

His hand came down and once again I was hoisted aloft. A big round face, big as my body, confronted me across a wide expanse of shiny wood. The mouth opened wide, exposing closed teeth that were subtle shades of yellow, green and blue. The smells from him made me wary but didn't alarm me at all. He reached a great fat hand towards me and I sank my teeth into the soft flesh. Although I hadn't the strength really to hurt anyone yet, the hand was jerked away in surprise then returned to give me a firm cuff on the jaw. I shouted at him and tried to nip the offending hand again, but it began to weave in circles, teasing me by suddenly tapping my nose. Now a dog's nose is a sensitive area, and I began to get really angry. I shouted at him again and he roared mockingly at me, increasing his taps to a very annoying degree. My protector seemed quite happy to let this stranger irritate me, for I sensed no nervousness in him at all. Pretty soon, my whole world was focused on that moving lump of flesh and I lunged my head forward hopefully.

This time, my pointed little teeth sank into the meat and I crunched down, hard as I could. The taste wasn't much but the satisfaction was exquisite. Even though the hand was wrenched from my grasp, I had the pleasure of seeing tiny pinpricks of blood in a neat row across three fingers, and the short howl of pain excited me even more. I yapped defiantly at the creature as he shook his stinging paw in the cold air. He made as though to lunge at me and I was whisked smartly away by my giant. Once again I found myself on the floor, small and vulnerable among the massive figures around me. Curiously, the sharp roaring sound from above had a quality to it that bespoke friendliness; I was beginning to recognise the sound of laughter from the other noises these big animals made.

Still puzzled by everything that had happened to me that day, and still trembling with the excitement of it all, I spread my legs and urinated on the floor. The puddle spread beneath me and I had to shift slightly to prevent my feet getting wet. This time, although many of the sounds that reached me were of this happy nature, there were others that alarmed me terribly. I felt a blow to my flank, sharp growls, then I was dragged by my neck across the vast cavern. The sun hit my eyes, blinding me after the gloom, and the giant crouched beside me, stern sounds coming from him, his finger waving in front of my nose. I tried to bite the finger, of course, but a hard thump across my withers told me this would be the wrong thing to do. I felt utterly miserable again and my tail dropped between my legs. The giant must have sensed my dejection, because his tone softened and once again I was riding high, snug against his chest.

As he walked, a new sensation reached me. It was a fresh sound in my inner ear and I looked up in surprise. The giant's mouth had formed a curious round circle and he was blowing air through it, making an appealing, high-pitched noise. I watched him for a few seconds then called out encouragement. Abruptly the noise ceased and he looked down. I sensed his pleasure and the noise continued. The whistling had a soothing effect on me and I settled down on his arm, my rump supported in the crook of his elbow, his fingers spread across my brisket, and my head against his heart. I began to feel drowsy.

It was just as well I felt tired, since the next stage in my traumatic journey was inside one of those mammoth red creatures. I realised now that the things were not living animals like the giant and me; but they were all the more disconcerting for it. However, my sleepiness overcame my fear and I half slept on his lap for most of the journey.

My next memory is that of a long drab grey road with equally grey drab houses on either side. I didn't know what houses – or roads, for that matter – were at that time, of course; to me, the world was full of strange shapes which had no identity or particular relevance. I learned fast, however, because I was unique; most animals accept rather than learn.

He stopped and pushed a wooden caging that reached as high as his waist. A section of it opened and he marched along a hard fiat surface, surrounded by beautiful green fur. The multitoned greenness dazzled my eyes and I was aware that this fur was a living, breathing thing. One hand reached inside his skin and emerged with a thin-looking object. He put this into a tiny hole in the structure before him and gave it a quick twist. A rectangular shape, sharp-cornered, taller than both of us, and coloured a vivid brown (even deep brown can be vivid when you see things as I do), swung inwards and we entered my first real home as a dog.

Three

I didn't stay there long.

Those early months are a confusing blur to me. I suppose my freakish brain was trying to adjust to its new existence. I remember being placed in a basket which I refused to stay in; I remember strange white flimsy things placed on the floor all around me; I remember the lonely darkness of night.

I remember being shouted at, my nose being rubbed in foul-smelling puddles – and worse, nasty, sticky stuff, the smell of which clung to my nostrils for hours afterwards. I remember torn and mangled articles waved in front of me, the giant's companion screeching hysterically. I remember an excitingly smelly place, the mingled scents of many creatures blending into a sniffer's paradise, where an ogre in a loose, white skin stabbed me with a long, thin object, pressing it into my back and holding it there while I yelped. I remember an annoying length of dried skin being fastened round my neck, occasionally joined to a longer piece which the giant held and used to drag me along or hold me back when we were out in the open. I remember my dread of the big non-animal creatures that would chase us but lose interest and speed by with snarling roars just as it seemed they would crush us to death.

If all this sounds as though I had a miserable time as a pup then it's not quite accurate. There were lovely moments of both comfort and exhilaration. I remember cosy evenings snuggled up on my keeper's lap in front of the wispy hot thing that scorched my nose when I tried to sniff it. I remember my coat being smoothed by the giant's hand, from the top of my head to the root of my tail. I remember my first introduction to the endless green fur that lived and breathed, and smelled so fragrant, so full of life itself. I ran, jumped, rolled in its softness; I chewed, sniffed, I positively wallowed in its abundance. I remember chasing the funny, sharp-eared thing who belonged to the creatures living on the other side of our wall, his fur sticking out from his body like thousands of needles, his tail ramrod straight, his mouth spitting obscenities at me. That was fun. I remember teasing my giant by grabbing one of the funny old pads he would cover his feet with, and making him run after me until he gave up in exasperation. I'd sidle up to him, place it on the ground before him, give a happy grin, then whisk it away before he had a chance to grab it. I remember the delicious scraps of food they would feed me; the food I refused to eat at first because it was so distasteful, but when hunger pains had overcome my repugnance, I'd eaten it with relish, saliva drooling from my clamping jaws. My own blanket, which I chewed and pawed until it became a tatty old thing, but which I refused to be parted from. My favourite bone, which I hid behind a bush in the little square green patch just outside our see-through wall. All these things I remember vaguely, but with nostalgic fondness.

I suppose I was a neurotic pup, but then you would be too, if you'd been through my experience. As indeed, you might.

I'm not sure just how long I stayed with the giant and his companion – I suppose it was three or four months at least. It was a doggy life for me, my human senses still dormant but ready to erupt at the slightest nudge. I'm thankful I was allowed to adapt to my new shell before the shattering knowledge burst through. The next stage wasn't far off though, and of course I was quite unprepared for it.

The reason for getting rid of me, I imagine, was because I was a pest. I know the giant liked me, even loved me in a way, for I can still remember his affection, *feel* his goodness, till this day. Those first terror-filled nights when I howled in the darkness for my brothers and sisters – my mother – he took me up to his sleeping-place. I slept on the floor beside him, much to the annoyance of his companion, and much to her even greater

20

annoyance when she discovered the damp patches and the soft, gooey mounds scattered around the spongy floor the following morning. I think that put me on the wrong side of her from the start. The relationship between us never really developed into anything more than wariness of each other. In due fairness to her, I think the best I can say is she treated me like a dog.

Words were only sounds to me then, but I could feel the emotion in them. I sensed, without understanding that I was a substitute for something else, and it's easy enough now to realise just what. They were, as far as I can remember, a mature couple, and they were alone. I could tell, from the noises the couple often made at each other, that the giant was full of shame and his mate full of scorn. I was confused enough as a pup and the atmosphere between them did nothing to help my emotional stability. Anyhow, as a substitute, I was no great success.

I don't know whether it was just one particular incident or an accumulation of disasters that led to my dismissal. All I know is that one day I found myself back among canine companions. My second home was a dogs' home.

And it was there that the breakthrough came.

Four

I'd been there for about a week, quite happy with my new friends, although a few were a bit rough. I was reasonably well fed (you had to fight for a fair share, though — a case of dog-eat-dog really), and quite well looked after. The big two-legged animals used to file past most days, calling down to us, making silly clucking noises, then pointing out one of us in particular. An older dog told me these creatures were called people, and it was they who governed everything; they ruled the world. When I asked what the world was, he turned away in impatient disgust and ran over to the people, sticking his nose through the wire grille in a show of homage. I soon learnt he was an old hand at the game of selection, for this wasn't his first visit to the dogs' home. I also learnt it wasn't a good thing not to be selected — eventually you would be taken away by a white-skin, and there was no mistaking the smell of death hanging over you.

The more experienced dogs told me about people: how they shed their skins at will, since it was only dead skin like the thing round my neck; how there were males and females, like us, and that they called their puppies children. If they kept repeating a sound to you, sometimes kindly, sometimes harshly, then that was probably your name. They would feed you and look after you if you were obedient. They had learned to walk on two legs a long, long time ago, and had felt superior ever since. They were a little stupid, but could be very kind.

They had the power to destroy *all* animals, even those bigger than themselves.

And it was that power, *and only that*, that made them the masters.

I discovered I was what was called a crossbreed – in other words, a mongrel. There's no class system among dogs, of course, but different breeds do have different characteristics. For instance, a labrador retriever is gentle and intelligent, whereas a greyhound is generally skittish and somewhat neurotic; you can hardly say a word to the latter without getting a snappish reply. It's funny how the dogs knew what they were: a terrier knew it was a terrier, a spaniel it was a spaniel. However, a Scottish terrier couldn't tell it was different from an Airedale; nor would a cocker spaniel know it was different from a clumber. These differences weren't important enough to be noticed.

Another point I soon discovered was that generally the bigger the dog, the more placid he or she was. It was the little squirts who caused the most trouble. And at that time, I was a little squirt.

I'd howl for my once-a-day meal; I'd whine against the blackness of night, I'd torment the sillier dogs, I'd wrestle the friskier ones. I'd snap and snarl at anyone who displeased me and I'd get very angry and chase the long thing that curled from my rump (I never caught it and it was quite a while before I accepted I never would). Even the fleas irritated me, and if I saw one hopping about on a companion's back I'd lunge for it, nipping the other dog's flesh. This would usually create a fine din and pretty soon a white-skin would throw a cold-making liquid over our struggling bodies.

I was soon earmarked as a troublemaker, often finding myself separated from the rest in a cage of my own. This made me even more morose and irritable and pretty soon I felt very unloved. The people just didn't realise: I had problems!

The problems were of course buried deep inside me where a strange conflict was going on. I knew I was a dog; yet instincts, senses – call it intuition – told me I wasn't. The conflict erupted to the surface on a cold, dream-filled night.

I had been asleep on the fringe of a group of furry bodies that had closed their ranks on me – I wasn't very popular with the other canines by that time – and my head was full of strange

23

images. I was tall, precariously balanced on two legs, my face level with those of the people; a female people was walking towards me, kindness radiating from her, nice sounds coming from her jaws. I seemed to know her, and I wagged my tail, the motion almost unbalancing me. She made a soft sound that was familiar to me and her jaws formed a curious round shape. Her head was only inches away from mine and coming closer, making contact. My tongue snaked out and licked her nose.

She pulled back, a tiny sound escaping from her. I could tell she was surprised by her sudden body smell. She became even more surprised when I started panting and wagging my tail even harder. She backed away and I followed unsteadily on my two back legs.

She began to run and now I had to drop on all fours to follow. Colours, sounds and scents cascaded into my head, and all was chaos, all was confusion. Other faces appeared before me. One was tiny, beautiful, a little female people — a child. She rubbed her head against mine, then climbed up on my back, kicking her legs against my flanks. We frolicked on the green stuff and I felt I would burst with joy. Then darkness shadowed the sky. Another face. Anger glowing from it. I disappeared and I was in a cage. In the market-place. Then I was in among other warm bodies which froze, went icy cold when the dogs opened their eyes and saw me.

Then all was total blackness.

But I was safe. I was warm. A loud, comforting thumping noise sounded close to me, almost inside me. Other, less strong sounds ticked away furiously all around. Everything, everywhere, was soft; I was encased in life-giving, life-preserving fluid. I was in my mother's womb and I was content.

Then the driving force behind me — the sudden brutal jerks of contraction. I was being forced from my safe nest, thrust down a long black tunnel into the harsh cold of the outside. I resisted. I wanted to stay. I'd known that outside before. I didn't like it. Please, please let me stay! Don't send me out. I don't want life. Death is more pleasant.

But the forces were so much stronger than me. Death had been stronger, and now life was too.

My head was pushed through first, and for a moment my small body lingered. There were others in the queue though, and they forced me through, eager in their ignorance. I shivered and my eyes refused to open: reality would find me in its own time. I felt the other glistening wet bodies around me, then a sand-paper-rough tongue cleansed the filth from me and I lay there, humble and vulnerable.

Reborn.

I screamed and the scream woke me.

My head felt as if it would explode with the new knowledge. I wasn't a dog; I was a *man*. I had existed before as a man and somehow I had become trapped inside an animal's body. A dog's body. How? And why? Mercifully the answers evaded me; if they hadn't, if they had come roaring through at that point, I think I should have become insane.

My scream had woken the other dogs and now the pen was a bedlam of excited barking. They snapped and snarled at me, but I just stood there shivering, too dazed to move. I knew myself as a man, I could see myself. I could see my wife. I could see my daughter. Images rebounded around the walls of my mind, merging, splitting, rejoining, bedevilling me into a state of complete disorientation.

Suddenly the place was flooded with light. I squeezed my eyes shut to ease the pain and opened them again when I heard men's voices. A door opened and two white-skins stepped through, grumbling and shouting at the disturbed dogs.

'It's that little bugger again,' I heard one of them say. 'He's been nothing but trouble since he got here.'

A hand reached down and grabbed me roughly. My collar was used to drag me from the pen and down a long corridor of similar cages, the dogs in these now yapping furiously, adding to the uproar. I was shoved into a dark box, a kennel separated from the others to house nuisances. As the door was locked behind me I heard one of the men say, 'I think he'll have to be put down tomorrow. Nobody's going to want a mongrel like that anyway, and he's only upsetting the others.'

I didn't hear the murmured reply, for the words had struck new terror in me. I was still confused by the awful revelation, but the brutal statement had cut right through the haze. Standing there, rigid in the dark with my mind in a fever, I began to weep. What had happened to me? And why was my new life to be so short? I slumped to the floor in despair.

Soon, other instincts began to take over; my jumbled self-pitying thoughts began to take on an order. I had been a man, there was no doubt about that. My mind was that of a man's. I could understand the words the two men had spoken, not just their general meaning, but the actual words themselves. Could I speak? I tried, but only a pathetic mewing noise came from my throat. I called out to the men, but the sound was just a dog's howl. I tried to think of my previous life, but when I concentrated, the mental pictures slid away. How had I become a dog? Had they taken my brain from my human body and transplanted it into the head of a dog? Had some madman conducted a gruesome experiment and preserved a living brain from a dying body? No, that couldn't be, for I had remembered being born in my dream, born in a litter, my mother-dog washing the slime from my body with her tongue. But had that merely been an illusion? Was I really the result of a sick operation? Yet if that had been the case, surely I would be under constant surveillance in a well-equipped laboratory somewhere, my whole body wired to machines, not cast into this gloomy wooden dungeon.

There had to be an explanation, whether logical or completely insane, and I would seek out the truth of it. The mystery saved my mind, I think, for it gave me a resolve. If you like, it gave me a destiny.

The first need was for me to calm myself. It's strange now to reflect on how coldly I began to think that night, how I held the frightening – the awesome – realisation in check, but shock can do this sometimes; it can numb sensitive brain cells in a self-protective way, so that you're able to think logically and clinically.

I wouldn't force my memory to tell me all its secrets just yet –

it would have been impossible anyway. I'd give it time, allow the fragments to make a whole, helping the images by searching, searching for my past.

But first I had to escape.

Five

The latch being lifted aroused me from my slumber. It had been a heavy sleep; empty; dreamless. I suppose my fatigued brain had decided to close down for the night, give itself a chance to recuperate from the shocks it had received.

I yawned and stretched my body. Then I became alert. This would be my chance. If they were to destroy me today, I must make my move while they were off-guard. When they came to take me to the death chamber, their own sensitivity to the execution they were about to carry out would make them wary. It's easy for humans to transmit their feelings to animals, you see, for their auras radiate emotions as strong as radio waves. Even insects can tune in to them. Even plants. The animal becomes sensitive to his executioner's impulses and reacts in different ways: some become placid, quiet, while others become jittery, hard to handle. A good vet or animal keeper knows this and endeavours to disguise his feelings in an effort to keep the victim calm; but they're not successful usually and that's when there's trouble. My hope was that this visit was social and not for the more ominous purpose.

A young girl of about eighteen or nineteen wearing the familiar white smock of the handlers looked in. She just had time to say 'Hello, boy' before I caught the whiff of sadness from her, then I was off like a shot. She didn't even try to grab me as I dashed by; she was either too startled or secretly pleased I was making a bid for freedom.

I skidded, trying to turn aside from the pound opposite and my toenails dug into the hard ground. My whole body was a scrambling mass of motion as I streaked around the half-covered yard, searching for a way out. The girl gave chase but in a half-hearted way as I scurried from corner to corner. I found a door to the outside world, but there was no way to get through it. I was filled with frustration at being a dog; if I'd been a man, it would have been easy to draw the bolt and step outside. (Of course, I wouldn't have been in that position then.)

I turned to growl at the girl as she approached, soft, coaxing words coming from her lips. My hair bristled and I went down on my front legs, my haunches quivering with gathering strength. The girl hesitated and her sudden doubt and wear wafted over me in waves.

We faced each other, and she felt sorry for me and I felt sorry for her. Neither of us wanted to frighten the other.

A door opened in the building at the far end of the yard and a man appeared, an angry look on his face.

'What's all the fuss, Judith? I thought I told you to bring the dog from Kennel Nine.' His expression changed to one of exasperation when he saw me crouching there. He strode forward, muttering oaths under his breath. I saw my chance – he'd left the door open behind him.

I hurtled past the girl, and the man, now half-way down the yard, spread his arms and legs as though I would jump into them. I passed underneath him and he vainly scissored his legs together, howling as his ankles cracked together. I left him hopping and flew through the open doorway, finding myself in a long, gloomy corridor, doors on either side. At the end was the door to the street, huge and formidable. Shouting from behind made me scurry down the corridor's length, desperate for a way out.

One of the doors on my left was slightly ajar, and without pausing I burst through. A woman on her knees just in the process of plugging in an electric kettle in the corner of the room stared across at me, too surprised to move. She began to rise to one knee and in panic I ran beneath a desk. My nose picked up the scent of fresh air mingled with dog fumes and, looking up, I saw an open window. A hand was reaching under the desk for me now and I could hear the woman's voice calling to me in friendly tones. I sprang forward, up on to the sill, then through the window.

Terrific. I was back in the yard.

The girl Judith saw me and called out to the man who had by now entered the building, but the yapping of the other dogs succeeded in drowning her cry. I kept running, back through the door and up behind the man chasing me.

He shouted in confusion as I scurried round him, and gave chase immediately. I was sure they'd have the sense to close one of the outlets if I went through my door-window-door routine again, so I ignored the open office. I found an alternative: facing the heavy street door was a flight of stairs, broad and dark-wooded. I did a scrambled U-turn and flew up them, my little legs pumping away like piston-rods. The man began mounting the stairs behind me and his long, long legs gave him the advantage. He sprawled forward, arms reaching upwards and I felt my progress abruptly halted by an uncompromising grip on my right hind leg. I yelped in pain and tried to draw myself away and up. It was no use, I hadn't the power to escape from such a tight clutch.

The man pulled me down towards him in one strong wrench and grabbed me by the neck with his other hand. He released my leg and put his hand underneath me, lifting my body up against his chest. At least I had the satisfaction (even though it was unintentional) of peeing on him.

It was my good fortune that at that precise moment someone else decided to show up for work. Brilliant sunshine flooded into the hallway as the front door swung open and a man carrying a briefcase entered. He stared in surprise at the scene before him: the young girl and the woman from the office gazing anxiously up at the dancing, cursing man who held the struggling pup away from his body, trying desperately and failing miserably to avoid the yellow stream that jetted from it.

It was just the right time to bite my captor's hand and, with a twist of my neck, I managed to do so. My jaws weren't that strong yet, but my teeth were like needle-points. They sank into his flesh and went deep – deep as I could make them. The sudden shock of pain caused the man to squawk and release his grip on me; I suppose the combination of wetness at one end and burning fire at the other offered him no other alternative. I fell to the stairs and tumbled down them, yelping with fright rather than hurt. When I reached the bottom, I staggered to my feet, gave my head a little shake, and bolted into the sunlight.

It was like bursting through a paper hoop from one dark, depressing world into a neighbouring world of brightness and hope. It must have been the taste of freedom that exalted me so, the gloom of the building I had just left contrasting with the brilliance of the sun and the exciting multifarious scents of life on the outside. I was free and the freedom lent vigour to my young limbs. I fled and wasn't pursued; nothing on this earth could have caught me anyway. The taste of life was in me and questions pounded my brain.

I ran, and ran, and ran.

Six

I ran till I could run no more, shying away from passing cars, ignoring the entreaties from the bemused or curses from the startled, nothing on my mind but escape – freedom. I had streaked across roads, blind to the danger because of the worse fear of capture, and had found quieter refuge in the back-streets; yet still I did not decrease my pace, still my feet drummed on the concrete pavements. I fled into the courtyard of an ancient, red-bricked block of flats, its redness darkened by the grime, and came to a quivering body-heaving halt inside a dark stairwell. My tongue flapped uselessly below my lower jaw, my eyes bulged with still unshed fright, my body sagged with utter weariness. I had run for at least two miles without pause, and for a young pup that's quite a distance.

I sank to the cold stone floor and tried to let my muddled brain catch up with my still dancing nerves. I must have lain there, a boneless heap, for at least an hour or more, too exhausted to move, too fuddled to think, the previous elation dissipated with dispersed energy, when the sound of heavy footsteps made me jerk my head up, my ears twitching for more information. I hadn't realised until then how acute my hearing had become, and it took long, long seconds for the owner of the footsteps to come into view. An immense figure blocked out most of the light infiltrating the dark stairwell, and in silhouette I saw the round shape of an enormous woman. To say her bulk filled the whole of my vision, periphery and all, may sound an exaggeration, but that's how it seemed to me in my shrunken body. It was as though her grossness were about to envelop me, to roll over me so that I would come up again, flattened to her side, just another added layer to the multitude of other layers. I cringed and I grovelled, no defiant pride in me, no sense of manhood available to hinder my cowardice for I was no longer a man. But her words halted my rising fear.

'Hello, boy, what you doing there, then?' The voice was as expansive as her body, booming and raspy, but the words were full of goodness and delighted surprise. She lowered her crammed shopping-bags to the floor with a grunt, then bent her vast upper structure towards me.

'Now, where've you come from, eh? Lost are you?'

Her gravelly tones suggested London, probably East or South. I backed away from the approaching hand even though my fear had been subdued by the quality of her voice; I knew once within the grip of those big, sausage-fingered hands, no amount of struggling would free me. But the lady was patient and undemanding. And the delicious aroma from those puffy fingers was overwhelming.

I sniffed small, tentative sniffs, nose-twitching sniffs, then inhaled deep lungfuls, the juices beginning to flow in my mouth. I flicked out my tongue and almost rolled my eyes in ecstasy. What this woman must have eaten! I could taste bacon, beans, tangy meat I couldn't identify, cheese, bread, butter – oh, butter – marmalade (not so nice), onions, tomatoes, another kind of meat (beef, I think) – and more, more, more. A taste of earthiness tainted everything, almost as if she had collected potatoes fresh from the ground, but it failed to sicken me as it should; instead, it heightened the deliciousness of it all. Here was a person who believed in food, who worshipped it with her hands as well as her palate; no stainless steel instruments would delay the journey from plate to munching jaws when the trip could be accomplished faster and with a heavier load by using her own living flesh to transport the goods. I could feel my devotion growing with every lick.

Only when the fat hand had been completely licked free of all its flavours did I turn my attention fully to the rest of the woman.

Dark blue eyes grinned down at me from a wide, rusty face. Rusty? Oh yes, you'd be surprised at the colours in faces if you could only see them as I did then. Red and blue veins coursed

33

through plump, flushed cheeks, just beneath the skin. Other colours glowed from her – yellows and oranges mostly – changing hues constantly as her blood circulated beneath the surface. Brown and grey hairs stood out from her chin like tiny porcupine quills; and over the whole countenance ran deep grooves, starting at the corners of each eye and spreading down and around the cheeks, up and over the forehead, twisting and merging, cross-hatching and fading to a gradual end. It was a wonderful face!

I saw all this in the gloom of the stairwell, remember, and with the light behind her. That's how powerful my new vision was and would have remained had not time organised and dulled it.

She clucked her tongue and gave a little laugh. 'You're a hungry little thing, aren't you? You know me, though, don't you? You know I'm a friend.'

I allowed her hand to ruffle the fur at the back of my neck. It was soothing. I sniffed fresh food from the shopping-bags and edged towards them, my nose twitching inquisitively.

'Oh, smell food, do you?'

I nodded. I was starving.

'Well, let's just see if there's anyone about that might have lost you.'

She straightened up and lumbered back towards the entrance and I trotted after her. We both stuck our heads out into the courtyard and looked around. It was deserted.

'Come on then, let's see what we can find.'

The old woman turned back into the gloom, hoisted her shopping-bags with a loud grunt and carried them down the short hallway behind the stairwell, calling encouragingly to me as she went. I padded after her and muscle movement in my rump told me my tail was wagging.

Placing the bags on the floor next to a badly worn green door, she produced a purse from her coat and rummaged through it until she found a key, cursing her failing eyesight. She opened the door with a hard shove and a practised twist of the key, reached again for her bags, and disappeared inside. I ambled cautiously up to the door and poked my nose round it. The musty smell that hit me was neither pleasant nor unpleasant; it told of old-age neglect.

'Come on, boy,' the woman called out, 'nothing to be frightened of. You're all right with Bella.'

Still I did not enter the room. My nervousness had not yet completely disappeared. She patted her knee in enticement, not an easy thing to do for one of her proportions, and without further thought I skipped towards her, my tail now causing the whole of my rump to vibrate.

'There's a good boy,' she rasped, and now I could understand words and not just feel them, I knew I really was a very good boy.

I forgot myself and tried to speak to her then; I think I wanted to tell her how kind she was and ask her if she knew why I was a dog. But of course I only barked.

'What's that, then? You hungry? Course you are! Let's see what we can find then.'

She went through a door and soon I heard the clatter of cupboards opening and closing. The deep, scratchy sound of her voice puzzled me for a few seconds, then I realised Bella was singing, an occasional word interrupting a series of monotone 'mmms' and 'laaas'.

The crackle of frying fat took my attention and the glorious smell of sausages beginning to cook sucked me into the kitchen like dust into a vacuum cleaner. I jumped up at her, resting my front paws against a broad leg, my feverishly wagging tail threatening to unbalance me. She smiled down at my excited whimpers and placed a huge hand over my head.

'Poor old thing. Won't be a minute now. I suppose you'd like them raw, wouldn't you? Well you just wait a couple of minutes and we'll share them between us. Now get down and be patient.' She gently pushed me away but the savoury smell was too much. I jumped up at the cooker and tried to see into the frying-pan.

'You'll burn yourself!' she scolded. 'Come on, let's put you out of harm's way until it's ready.' She scooped me up and lumbered over to the kitchen door where she dropped me with a soft grunt. I tried to squeeze through the narrowing gap as the door closed on me but had to withdraw when my nose was in jeopardy. I'm ashamed to say I whined and groaned and scratched at the kitchen door, my thoughts concerned only with filling my belly with those mouth-watering sausages. Questions of my bizarre existence were thrust aside, easily overwhelmed by the stronger, physical desire for food.

Finally, after what seemed an eternity of waiting, the door opened and a cheery voice called me in. I needed no second bidding; I streaked through and made a bee-line for the plate containing three powerful-smelling sausages. I yelped as the first I snapped at burnt my tongue, and the old lady chuckled at my greedy attempts to bite the sizzling meat. I'd picked one up and immediately dropped it on to the floor when it stung my mouth. I did manage to swallow a chunk but it scorched my throat painfully. Bella thought it wiser to take the sausages away from me and, annoyed, I yapped at her.

'You just be patient,' she reprimanded. 'You'll do yourself an injury with these.'

Gingerly she picked up the sausage I'd already bitten into and blew on it – long, strong puffs that defied the sizzling heat to resist it. When she was satisfied she popped the sausage into my upturned mouth. In two quick swallows it was gone and I was pleading for more. She went through the ritual again, ignoring my impatient entreaties. I appreciated the second even more, the savoury meat filling my mouth with its juices, and, I can honestly say, never had I enjoyed a meal so much in my life – lives – either as a dog or as a man.

When I had gulped down the third, the old lady turned her attention back to the frying-pan and stabbed out four more sausages with a fork, placing two each on a slice of thick bread lying on the table. She smeared them with mustard and covered them with another slice, almost tenderly, as if putting a couple of children to bed. Without bothering to cut it she opened her jaws and stuffed as much of the sausage sandwich into her mouth as possible. Her teeth clamped down and when she withdrew her hand, a huge semicircular hole had been left in the bread. I watched enviously and tried to jump up on to her lap, the sight of those huge munching jaws sending me into a frenzy of pleading. I was starving! Didn't she have any pity?

She laughed and ruffled my head, holding me at bay, keeping the sandwich well away from my snapping teeth. I was in luck, for a lump of sausage fell from the bread and I was on it in an instant. I licked my lips with pleasure as I looked up for more.

'All right, you villain. I suppose it'll do you more good than me.' Bella smiled, and with that she dropped the rest of the sandwich on to the plate on the floor.

So we feasted, me and the fat lady, happy in each other's company, both of us demolishing our piece of sausage sandwich in seconds, grinning and smacking our lips at each other when we'd done.

I was still hungry, but at least the edge had been taken off my appetite. I lapped up the water Bella gave me in a soup-bowl and licked the traces of food from her hands. I asked for more but she didn't understand. She hoisted herself to her feet and began to unpack her shopping-bag while I kept a wary eye out for any scraps that might fall to the floor. It was risky dodging between those two wonderfully stout legs, and no food fell my way, anyway, but I enjoyed the game.

Bella dropped my spotless plate into the sink and called to me to follow her. I padded after her into her front-room and scrambled up on to the musty old settee as she sank into it with a groan. I jumped up at her chest, two paws placed between two massive breasts, and licked her face in gratitude. It was a pleasing face to lick. She stroked my head and back for a little while and the strokes became slower and heavier as her breathing became slower and heavier.

It was not long after Bella had lifted those great tree-trunks on to the settee and rested her head on a cushioned arm that she was fast asleep, her snoring strangely comforting to me. I curled up my own weary body between her mountainous tummy and the back of the settee and soon I was deep in slumber too.

My awakening was fairly alarming. I heard a key in the lock and was instantly alert. I tried to stand, but my legs were wedged firmly inside the crevice between the old lady and the settee. I lifted my head and began to bark as loud as I could. This startled Bella into wakefulness and she looked around for a few moments as though she didn't know where she was.

'The door, Bella.' I told her. 'There's someone coming in!'

She didn't understand, of course, and gruffly told me to hush my barking. I was too young though, too easily excited, and my barks only got louder and more challenging.

A man staggered in and fumes of alcohol assailed me. I had been into pubs a few times with my previous master and had always found the smell of alcohol unpleasant but not disturbing. However, this had the smell of sickness.

'What the bloody 'ell's that?'

The man lurched towards us. He was fairly young, about thirty, thirty-five, prematurely balding, his face vaguely containing the same features as Bella's. His clothes were untidy but not dishevelled; he wore no shirt, just a loose-fitting sweater under his jacket. Just as Bella was broad and expansive, he was small and mean. A giant, to me, of course, but a small, mean giant.

'Haven't you been in to work again?' Bella asked, still drawing her sleepy wits together.

He ignored the question and made a grab for me, a horrible sneer distorting his lips. I growled and snapped at his hand; I didn't like him at all.

'Leave the dog alone!' Bella pushed his hand away and heaved her legs on to the floor, causing me to fall back into the space she'd just vacated.

'Dog? Call that a dog?' He cuffed my head with malicious playfulness. I warned him not to do it again. 'Where'd he come from? You know you're not allowed dogs in the flats.'

'Leave him be. I found him outside – starving, he was, poor little thing.'

Bella rose, towering above me and dwarfing the weasel I supposed was her son. 'You stink,' she told him, standing between us to stop his teasing. 'What about your job? You can't keep taking time off like this.'

The weasel cursed his job then his mother. 'Where's me dinner?' he asked.

'The dog's had it.'

I groaned inwardly. That should endear me to him.

'He bloody better not have!'

'I didn't know you'd be home, did I? I thought you'd gone off to work.'

'Well, I haven't, so find me something.'

I think she should have picked him up by the scruff of the neck and stuck his head in a bucket of water – she was big enough to do so – but instead she marched off into the kitchen, and soon the sounds of cupboard doors opening and closing reached our ears.

He leered down at me and I glared nervously back at him.

'Off!' he commanded, jerking his thumb away from the settee.

'Get lost,' I replied with more coolness than I actually felt.

'I said *off*!' He lunged and swept me from my comfortable perch with a strength that petrified me. I still had to learn I was only a dog, and a pretty feeble one at that. I yelped in dismay and scooted off into the kitchen, seeking protection from Bella.

'All right, boy, all right. Take no notice of him. Let's give him his dinner and he'll soon be off to sleep, don't you worry.' She busied herself preparing the weasel's meal while I kept as close to her as possible. The food odours began to arouse my palate again and suddenly I was just as hungry as before. I rested my paws against her broad flank and begged to be fed again.

'No, no. You get down now!' Her hand was more firm than before. 'You've had your dinner, it's his turn now.'

Still I persisted, but Bella ignored my whines. She began to talk to me, maybe to soothe me, or perhaps she was really talking to herself.

'Takes after his father. Never no good, but what do you do? They're flesh and blood. He could've been something, that boy, but he's wasted himself. Just like the old man, God rest him, same blood in 'em. I've done me best, God knows I've done me best. Kept him – kept 'em both – when they were out of work. They've made me old, they have, between 'em.'

The smell of cooking was making me delirious.

'He's had some nice girls too. Can't keep 'em, though. Run a mile when they find out what he's like. He'll never change. Arnold, it's nearly ready! Don't you go asleep!'

Bacon, eggs, more sausages. Oh God!

She began to butter bread at the kitchen table while I stayed rooted beneath the cooker, oblivious to the hot fat that spluttered and occasionally spat over. Bella brushed me out of the way with a leg and emptied the contents of the pan on to a plate. She put the plate on the table then clattered about for a knife and fork.

'Arnold! Your dinner's ready,' she called out. No reply. With an annoyed grunt and a determined look on her face Bella marched into the front room.

The dinner on the table beckoned to me.

It was unfortunate really that the chair previously occupied by Bella was still projecting out from the kitchen table. I clambered on to it, falling back down once but renewing my efforts with desperate eagerness, then rested my paws on the table-top. Bella could only have been out of the room for no more than a few seconds, but that's all it took for two slices of bacon and one and a half sausages to be devoured. I was saving the eggs till last.

My shriek of alarm joined Bella's shriek of dismay and the weasel's shriek of rage in a reverberating cacophony. I leapt from the chair just as the son lunged past his mother, claws out-stretched to throttle me. Fortunately Bella used her massive frame to block his path and he sprawled forward over her fleshy hip, tumbling on to the floor in a loose bundle as only drunks can.

But even Bella was cross with me. I could see those muscled forearms were going to deal out some heavy punishment, so I did my best to keep the kitchen table between us. She stepped round her floundering son and advanced on me. I waited till she was half-way round the table, my front legs down, chin almost touching the floor, haunches high and quivering, then I shot beneath the table, heading for the open doorway – and straight into the arms of the weasel.

He picked me up by the neck, using two hands and squeezed as he did so, and raised himself from the floor, his demonic face only inches away from mine. My squirming body made him even more unsteady on his feet and he fell forward against the table. What was left of his dinner went flying as my back legs scrabbled for support, and his buttered bread, tomato sauce and God-knows-what-else followed suit.

'I'll kill 'im!' was all I heard before I sank my teeth into his skinny nose. (I'll bet he's still got those two rows of indents on either side of his snout today.)

'Get 'ib boff,' he cried out to his mother, and I felt huge banana hands engulf me. Bella ripped me away from him and I had the pleasure of seeing red skid-marks down the length of his nose.

He clutched at it with both hands and howled, skipping on the spot in a sort of dance.

'Jesus, Jesus,' moaned Bella. 'You'll have to go now. I can't keep you now.'

She swept me out of the kitchen, shielding me with her body from her hopping son, lest he forget his pain for a moment and make a grab for me. I don't think I wanted to stay any more, so I hardly protested when the front door opened and I was dumped outside. A heavy hand descended upon me and gave me one long last stroke. 'Off you go now, go on, get away,' Bella said, not unkindly, and the door closed, leaving me alone again.

Even then, I lingered for a moment looking mournfully up at the door, but when it flew open and the weasel appeared, his nose a bloody protuberance and his body shaking with fury, I knew it wouldn't be healthy to stay any longer. So I scooted, and he scooted after me.

As an ally to speed, I think terror has it over rage; I soon left him far behind, anyway.

Blurred images again: cars, people, buildings, none of them focused, none of them very real. Only the overpowering scent from a lamp-post halted my flight. I skidded to a stop, my back legs overtaking my front legs, and executed a clumsy turnabout. I trotted back to this ambrosial column, senses keen, nose twitching inquisitively. Of all the smells that had recently come to me, this was by far the most interesting. It was dog, you see, dog in the plural. There were six or seven different personalities wafting from the base of that concrete structure – not to mention a couple of human smells – and I drank them in giddily. I had sniffed trees and lamp-posts before, but now it seemed my senses were wakening afresh, or perhaps they were just heightening. I could almost *see* the dogs that had visited this towering urinal, almost *speak* to them; it was as if they'd left a recorded message for me. I could even detect the female of the species, and that, I think, has a lot to do with the dogs' interest in each other's pee: the sexual instinct, the search for a mate. The girls and the boys had left their calling cards as if to say: I've been here, this is my route; if you're interested, I may pass this way again. I was too young to be disturbed by any sexual connotation at that time, the rank yet spicy odours interesting me on a different level. They were company.

When my nose had been satiated I began to sniff my way along the pavement, oblivious to the passers-by, lost in the pursuit of intriguing trails. It was not long before sounds even more intriguing reached my ears. They were just a babble at first, like the clacking of excited geese, but as I drew nearer to their source, they took on a distinctly human quality. I quickened my pace, elation beginning to rise in me, the sounds sending out attracting waves of excitement.

Reaching a broad river of road I hesitated before dashing across and, fortunately, no dragons bore down on me. The sounds were now clamorous in my ears and, turning a corner, I fell upon their origin: an enormous expanse of running, jumping, shouting, screaming, giggling, crying, playing children. I had found a school. My tail launched into its self-motorised wagging and I sprang forward, thrusting my narrow head between the railings surrounding the playground.

A group of small girls spotted me and gleefully ran over, their hands reaching through the iron bars to pat my back. They screamed in delight as I tried to nip any fingers that tried to stroke my head; my intention wasn't to bite them, but to taste their soft flesh, to savour them. Soon, a large group of both boys and girls had formed a semicircle around my protruding head, the bigger boys pushing themselves forward through the crowd. Toffees were thrust into my eager mouth and fingers hastily withdrawn when it seemed I would swallow them too. A tiny girl with sunshine hair pushed her face close to mine and my tongue made her nose and cheek glistening wet. She didn't pull away, though, she hugged my neck.

And then fickle memories returned to taunt me. I had owned one of these! I almost thought this one was mine, she was the child who had belonged to me, but different features swam into vision. The hair was the same, a bright halo around an urchin face, but my daughter's eyes had been blue and the eyes that now smiled into mine were brown. A cry of hopefulness escaped me and the girl mistook it for one of fear. She tried to soothe me over the clamour of the other children, pleading with me not to be afraid, but my mind was paralysed with one thought. I was a man! Why was I living as a dog?

Then the paralysis wore off as the realisation slipped back into its hidden crevice and once again, in essence, I was a dog. (Although the disturbing fact that I was really a man never left me in those early months, because of the conflict of also being a dog, my humanness played a very varying degree of importance.)

My tail began its flag-waving again and I gratefully accepted more sweets. The kids fussed over me and tried to discover my name by calling out possibilities and waiting to see if I reacted to any. For the life of me I couldn't remember what I'd been called before, and the boys found nothing inscribed on my collar. Rover, King, Rex, Turdface (*Turdface!* What little horror threw that one in?) – I beamed at them all. Names meant nothing to me, nor do they to any dog – they recognise particular sounds. I was just happy to be among friends.

A sharp whistle shrilled through my ears and a loud moan went up from the children. Reluctantly, and only after a few sharper blasts from the whistle, they turned away and left me, my shoulders pressed hard up against the railings in an effort to follow. Sunshine Hair stayed till last and gave my neck a long, hard squeeze before departing. I woofed at them not to go, but they stood in rows with their backs to me, occasionally sneaking a look round, their shoulders jerking in suppressed giggles. Then, row by row, they filed into a miserable grey building and the door was closed behind the last one.

I stared blankly into the empty playground, distressed that I'd lost my new friends. I grinned and straightened up as little white faces appeared at upstairs windows, but these were soon joined by the older, wizened face of a teacher whose harsh, muffled voice carried across the playground, ordering the pupils to return to their seats. A boy who was slower than the rest got his ear tweaked as encouragement. I stayed there for a few more hopeful minutes, but finally, and mournfully, I tugged my head loose from the railings.

Dogs generally have happy spirits, and most emotions are

43

sacrificed to inquisitiveness anyway, so when an old man cycled by with a shopping-bag dangling from his handlebars, I forgot my disappointment and trotted along after him. I could see a leafy sprig protruding from a hole in the base of his shopping-bag. I think it must have been rhubarb – it had a sweet tangy smell – and it looked very appetising. I soon caught up with him, for he was quite old and peddling very slowly, and before he had a chance to notice me I leapt up at the tantalising sprig. I was both lucky and unlucky.

I pulled the leaf and its stalk through the hole, but the sudden action unbalanced the cyclist and he came crashing down on top of me, machine and all. The breath was knocked from me so that my yelp of pain was only a crushed squeal. I spluttered for air and tried to apologise to the old man for bringing him down, but my words emerged as a series of wheezy grunts which he didn't understand. He flailed his arms around, trying to hit me, not even *trying* to sympathise with my hunger, cursing and groaning as if he'd been tossed by a bull on to a bed of nails. And I'd managed to break his fall too!

There was no point in my staying, he wasn't in the mood to offer me any food, so I tried to struggle free of both man and machine. A few hefty clouts from him helped me considerably and I was delighted to discover the contents of the shopping-bag had scattered along the pavement. I ignored the long red stalks whose brief taste of foliage hadn't excited me tremendously and dashed at a juicy looking red apple. My jaws clamped down on it – not an easy feat, for it was a large apple – and then I scampered out of range of angry fists and abusive language. It was fortunate his feet were tangled up in the bike frame otherwise I'm sure they'd have been used to send me on my way. At a safe distance, I turned and dropped the apple on the ground before me. I had meant to apologise again for I did feel sorry I'd caused the man to fall and hurt himself, but his purple face and shaking fist convinced me he wouldn't be pacified. So, picking up my apple, I made off, looking back once to see him being lifted to his feet by two passers-by. He seemed all right as he hobbled around testing his aged legs, so I continued on my way.

I found a reasonably quiet side-street and settled down against a wall to eat my plunder. My appetite never seemed to be satiated in those early days and those 'experts' who tell you dogs need only one meal a day are talking through their hats. Certainly a dog only *needs* one meal a day to get by, but then, so does a human. How would you feel if that's all you had? And how would you feel if you had to fast for one day a week, something the 'experts' also recommend? What's the use of a glossy coat and a damp nose if you've got a gnawing stomach? I wolfed that apple down, core and all, as if it was all I'd eaten that day. The sun beat down on me and I dozed off, forgetting my problems, drowsiness forcing me to accept what was.

One of those inevitable English summer showers aroused me and I automatically looked at my wrist to see what the time was. The sight of my thin, hairy dog's leg shocked me into reality. I trotted to my feet and shook myself, then looked around; it must have been mid-afternoon and I was hungry again.

I set off down the narrow street, investigating new smells as they came to me, chasing a beetle as it scurried across my path, calling hello to a dog being lead by a man on the other side of the street. The dog, a disdainful little corgi, ignored me and I just wasn't interested enough to make conversation. It slowly dawned on me as I trotted on that I needed a quiet safe place, somewhere I could rest and try to unscramble my jumbled thoughts. I needed food and I needed protection. Some kind of sympathy would have been welcome too.

But I didn't find it that day.

I pushed my rump back in the doorway to avoid the drizzling rain spattering against my nose and foreface. It had been an afternoon of wandering and wondering; the sun had been dimmed by the steady drizzle and the damp had made the people even more insulated. Earlier on, the streets had suddenly become crowded, overwhelming me with their congestion so that I could only cower miserably under a railway arch. After what seemed a long time, their numbers dwindled and I ventured forth again, but by now my spirits had caved in completely. My tail dropped between my legs and my eyes scarcely left the pavement in front of me. As the evening drew on and the light faded, my loneliness had increased to such an extent that I was tempted to go back to the dogs' home – the Return of the Prodigal, Lassie Comes Home. The thought of being put to sleep – murdered, I mean – wouldn't have deterred me. I would be good, I would play the underdog to its lowest level, and the keepers would forgive me, give me another chance to prove my worthiness to be an unworthy creature, to be just another dog. I couldn't remember where the hell the dogs' home was, though.

I gazed longingly up at lighted windows, yearning for company, drinking in the inviting smells, but the rain drove me on, searching and just not finding.

The hour was late now and, apart from the occasional swish of a passing car, the streets were cold and empty. I huddled in the doorway, and my wretched spirit huddled within me. Tiredness made my eyelids droop, only hunger keeping me awake. Questions invaded my misery.

This place wasn't familiar to me, yet I knew it was London. Was I from London? No, I wasn't from London. How did I know? I just knew. I had a memory of green fields, open space; a town, but not a big town. They had formed the greater part of my life, these fields and this town. Where were they? If only I could find them. And yet I knew this city, even if this particular district was unfamiliar. Had I worked in London? I had a sudden vision of a woman, in her late fifties, plump but not large, smiling and holding her arms out, and it seemed she held them out to me, calling a name that was soundless to my ears. Her head became that of a dog's, and was just as warm, just as affectionate, just as welcoming. My two mothers vanished from my mind and were replaced by the figure of a man, a man who appeared quite normal, handsome in a featureless way, and his environment was somehow different, not part of the scene I had just envisaged.

I hated him. Was it me?

My thoughts wearily wandered on, uncontrolled, undirected: the child again, obviously mine; the girl – young woman – certainly my wife; a house; a street, a muddy lane; a town. The name of the town almost came to me; the names of the girl and the child hovered behind a tissue-thin barrier; my own name was rising from ocean depths and about to break surface. But a car swished past and the names scattered like startled fish.

I watched the car's rear lights recede into the distance, twin reflections on the soggy road diminishing with them, suddenly reinforced by brake lights, and disappearing as the vehicle turned a corner (even that seemed familiar). I was alone again in an empty world and with an empty head. Then I saw the ghost.

Have you ever seen a ghost? Probably not. But have you ever seen a dog suddenly become alert, for no apparent reason, his ears cocked, his hair bristling? You'd undoubtedly think he's just heard something that's escaped your ears, somebody walking by the house, another dog barking somewhere far in the night: and many times you'd be right. But often, it's because he's aware of presence – a spirit. He won't always be alarmed, perhaps just disturbed; it depends largely on the nature of the ghost itself. It could be friendly or unfriendly.

Think I'm going a bit far now? Just wait till later.

The ghost drifted across the road towards me, a shadowy form, a wispy, vaporous figure. It didn't see me, or, if it did, it chose to ignore me, and as the shape drew nearer, I was able to distinguish a face, shoulders, and a part of a torso. The apparition seemed to be wearing a jacket, and I could certainly make out a shirt-collar and tie. Why wasn't it naked – why do astral bodies never seem to be naked? Don't ask me, I'm only a dog.

Now, I was disturbed, I admit it. There was nothing evil emanating from the spirit, I'm sure, but it was my first ghost both as a dog or as a man. My hair stood on end and my eyes widened. My mouth suddenly felt very dry. I was too frightened even to whine and the power to run had left me completely.

It had the saddest countenance I've ever seen, a face that had been made aware of the ills of mankind, had learned the first lesson in death. It passed by me, close enough to touch, and I could clearly see the rain drizzling through it. Then the spectre was gone, drifting off into the night, leaving me to wonder if my restless mind hadn't invented the whole thing. It hadn't, for I was to see many more of these wandering spirits, most with the same burden of sadness, unaware it was just a phase for them; but it was to be a long time before I discovered their meaning.

The experience drained me of what strength I had left and I fell into a deep undisturbed sleep.

Seven

Gentle nudging woke me.

I shifted my position and tried to ignore the prodding, but I was too cold to become comfortable again. My eyes opened of their own accord and I saw a big black dog hovering over me.

'Come on, squirt, don't let them find you napping there.'

I blinked my eyes furiously, now fully awake.

'Where did you get loose from, eh? Run away from home, or did they lose you on purpose?' The big dog grinned down at me.

I shivered and tottered to my feet. 'Who are you?' I asked, unable to stifle a yawn. I stretched stiff limbs, my front legs going down on the ground, my back pushing my rump into the air as far as it could go.

'Rumbo's what they call me. You got a name?'

I shook my head. 'I might have. I can't remember it, though.'

The dog regarded me silently for a few moments, then had a sniff around me.

'There's something funny about you,' he announced finally.

I gulped at the understatement. 'You don't seem like the other dogs I know either,' I said. And he wasn't, I could sense it immediately. He was somehow brighter, or un-doglike, or . . . more human.

'We're all different. Some are more dopey than others, that's all. But with you it's something else. You're definitely a dog, aren't you?'

I nearly blurted out my problems to him there and then, but he suddenly lost interest in that line of thought and directed my own on to a much more basic level. 'You hungry?' he asked.

Only ravenous, I thought, nodding my head sharply.

'Come on, then, let's go and find something.' He turned away and was off down the road at a brisk pace. I had to scamper to catch up with him.

He was a bony mongrel, about five or six years old, an amalgamation of several breeds. Imagine a Dalmatian without spots, just black all over, and without elegant lines, with turned-in toes, cow-hocked hindquarters, excessive angulation of the back legs (they stuck out backwards too far) and weak pasterns, then you'd have a fair impression of Rumbo. He certainly wasn't ugly – not to me anyway – but he wouldn't have won any prizes, either.

'Come on, pup!' he called over his shoulder. 'We don't want to be late for breakfast!'

I drew level with him and said breathlessly, 'Do you think we could stop for just a minute, I need to do something?'

'What? Oh yes, all right.' He stopped and I squatted on the ground before him. He turned away in disgust and trotted over to a nearby lamp-post, cocked his leg and relieved himself in a professional manner. 'You'll avoid accidents if you do it this way,' he called over, as I tried to shift a leg that was being threatened by a spreading puddle.

I smiled back feebly, grateful that the streets were fairly empty and no human could see me in this undignified pose. It was the first time I'd felt self-conscious about that sort of thing, a sign of the dog versus human instinct conflict that was going on inside me.

Rumbo came over and sniffed mine and I went over to the lamp-post and sniffed his. When we were both satisfied, we went on our way.

'Where are we going?' I asked him, but he ignored me, his step becoming faster, excitement tightening his movements. Then I caught the first whiff of food, and my attention was captured.

The roads were busier now, yet the noise and the bustle didn't seem to bother Rumbo at all. I stuck as close to him as possible, my shoulder occasionally bumping against his thigh. The roads still frightened me; the buses seemed like mobile blocks of flats and the cars like charging elephants. My supersensitive vision didn't help matters much, the blinding colours heightening my fears, but nothing seemed to bother Rumbo. He skilfully avoided

50

pedestrians and used crossings to negotiate the dangerous roads, always waiting for a human to cross first, then trailing behind him, with me trying to become an extension of his body.

We reached a thunderous place where, even though it was still early morning, there were masses of people, hustling, bustling, hurrying – worrying. The noise was deafening, with men shouting, lorries hooting and hand-pulled barrows grinding along the concrete. Rich scents filled the air – the tang of many different fruits, the more earthy smell of vegetables, raw potatoes. If it hadn't been for the apparent chaos, I would have believed I'd found Heaven.

We were in a market, not a street-market, but a covered wholesale market, where restaurateurs, fruiterers, street-traders – anyone who sold fruit, veg or flowers – came to buy their stock; where growers and farmers brought their goods; where lorries arrived from the docks laden with food bought from exotic countries, and trucks departed, full to bursting point, bound for different parts of the country, or back to the docks where their contents would be loaded on to ships; where voices were surly as barter took place, as credit was extended – even as debts were paid.

A burly man, red-faced, bull-necked, wearing a dirty once-white smock, lumbered past us, pulling a barrow piled high with precariously balanced boxes, all packed with greenish-yellow bananas. He sang at the top of his voice, stopping only to swear amiably at a passing workmate, unaware that a hand of bananas was about to topple from the top of his load. As it did so I started forward, but Rumbo barked sharply.

'Don't you dare,' he warned me. 'They'd skin you alive in this place if they caught you stealing.'

Someone shouted and the man stopped his barrow, looking back round the stacked boxes to see the stray bananas. He cheerfully walked back to them and threw them high on to his load. He spotted us as he returned to the barrow's handles and stopped to give Rumbo a hearty pat on his back. I think the pat would have broken my spine. My new friend wagged his tail and tried to lick the man's hand.

'Hello, boy. Brought a friend with you today, 'ave you?' the

51

market porter said, reaching out for me. I backed away; my young body was too tender for such rough treatment. The man chuckled and turned back to his barrow, resuming his tuneless tune.

I was puzzled by Rumbo's attitude: why had we come here if we couldn't sample the food?

'Come on,' he said, as if in answer, and we were off again, dodging round salesmen, porters and buyers, threading our way through the disorder, Rumbo receiving a welcome or a friendly pat now and again. Occasionally we would be shooed on, and once we had to avoid a malicious boot aimed at us, but generally my older companion seemed to be well-known and an accepted part of the scene. Rumbo must have been working at it for quite a long time, for animals – apart from rat-catching cats – aren't generally tolerated around food-markets, particularly strays.

A new overpowering smell reached my sensitive nostrils, easily defeating the tang of mixed fruit and vegetables, and much more enticing to my grumbling tummy: the smell of frying meat. I saw where Rumbo had been heading and raced ahead, leaping up at the high counter of the mobile snack-bar. It was much too high for me, and I could do no more than rest my front paws against it and look up expectantly. I couldn't see anything because of the overhanging counter, but the smell of frying wafted down over me.

Rumbo appeared quite angry when he arrived, and said through clenched teeth, 'Get down, squirt. You'll spoil everything.'

I obeyed reluctantly, not wanting to upset my new-found friend. Rumbo paced himself back so that he would be visible to the man behind the high counter and yipped a couple of times. A skinny old head peeked over the edge of the counter and broke into a yellow-toothed smile.

' 'Allo, Rumbo. 'Ow yer doin' today? 'Ungry belly, eh? Let's see what we can find yer.' The head disappeared from my view so I rushed to join Rumbo, excitement at the prospect of food elating me.

'Keep still, pup. Don't make a nuisance of yourself or we'll get nothing,' he scolded.

I did my best to remain calm, but when the man behind the

counter turned to face us, a juicy-looking sausage held between two fingers, it was too much for me. I jumped up and down in anticipation.

'What's this, then, brought a mate along? This ain't meals-on-wheels yer know, Rumbo, I can't start feedin' all yer mates.' The man shook his head disapprovingly at Rumbo, but nevertheless dropped the sausage between us. I made a grab for it, but my companion was quicker, snarling and gobbling at the same time – not an easy thing to do. He gulped the last morsel into his throat, smacked his thin lips with his tongue and growled. 'Don't take liberties, shrimp. You'll get your turn, just be patient.' He looked up at the man who was laughing at the pair of us. 'What about something for the pup?' Rumbo asked.

'I suppose yer want something for the pup now, do yer?' the man asked. His tired old eyes crinkled and his large hooked nose became even more hooked as his grin spread wide across his thin face. He was an interesting colour actually: yellow with deep mahogany etchings patterning his features, greasy but still some-how dry skinned, the oiliness being only on the surface. 'All right then, let's 'ave a look.' He turned away again and as he was about to find me something a voice called out, 'Cuppa tea, Bert.'

One of the porters leaned his elbows against the counter and yawned. He looked down at us and clicked his tongue in greeting. 'You wanna' watch this, Bert, you'll 'ave the inspectors after you if you 'ave too many of these 'anging about.'

Bert was filling a cup with deep brown tea from the most enormous metal teapot I'd ever seen.

'Yerse,' he agreed. 'It's usually the big one on 'is own. Brought a mate today though, probably one of 'is nippers, looks like 'im, dunnit?'

'Nah,' the porter shook his head. 'The big one's a proper mongrel. The little one's a crossbreed. Got a good bit of Labrador in 'im and . . . let's see . . . a bit of terrier. Nice little thing.'

I wagged my tail for the compliment and looked eagerly up at Bert.

'All right, all right, I know what you want. 'Er's yer sausage. Eat it and then scarper, you'll 'ave me licence.'

He threw the sausage down at me and I managed to catch it in mid-air; it burnt my tongue though and I had to drop it hastily. Rumbo was on it immediately. He bit it in half and swallowed. I pounced on the other half, but Rumbo stood back, allowing me to gulp it down. My eyes watered from the heat of it and I could feel its warmth working its way down my throat.

'Sorry, squirt, but you're here only because I brought you. You've got to learn respect.' Rumbo looked up at the snack-bar man, barked his thanks and trotted away from the stall.

I glanced at the two chuckling men, said my thanks, and chased after him.

'Where we going now, Rumbo?' I shouted.

'Keep your voice down,' he reprimanded, waiting so I could catch up. 'The trick is not to be conspicuous in a place like this. That's why they don't mind me coming in, because I behave myself, keep out of their way and . . . ' he looked meaningfully at me, seeing I was about to run after a rolling orange which had fallen from one of the display stands ' . . . and I *never* take anything unless it's offered to me.'

I ignored the orange.

We left the market, accepting half a black soggy banana each on our way, and skipped along into the less cluttered streets.

'Where are we going now?' I inquired again.

'We're going to steal some food now,' he answered.

'But you just said back . . . '

'We were guests there.'

'Oh.'

We found a butcher's on a busy main road. Rumbo stopped me and peeked round the open doorway. 'We've got to be careful here, I did this place last week,' he whispered.

'Er, look, Rumbo, I don't think . . . '

He hushed me up. 'I want you to go in there over to the far corner – don't let him see you till you get there.'

'Look, I'm . . . '

'When you're there, make sure he *does* see you, then you know what to do.'

'What?'

'You know.'

'I don't know. What do you mean?'

Rumbo groaned aloud. 'Save me from stupid mutts,' he said. 'Your business, you do your business.'

'I can't. I can't go in there and do that.'

'You *can*. You're *going* to.'

'But I'm not in the mood.' The thought of the danger had put me in the mood, though.

'You'll manage,' Rumbo said smugly. He sneaked a look back inside the shop. 'Quick, now's the time! He's cutting meat on his slab. Get in there, quick!'

He bustled me in, using his powerful jaws to nip my neck as encouragement. Now, I'm sure you've never seen two dogs act this way outside a butcher's shop before, but there aren't many dogs like Rumbo and me around, just the odd few. You've seen dogs mugging kids for their ice-creams and sweets, though, and I'm sure you've caught your own dog stealing at some time or other. What you haven't seen – or perhaps noticed – is organised canine crime. Most dogs are too stupid for it, but I can assure you it does exist.

I entered the shop and slunk along under the counter where the chopping butcher couldn't see me, looking back pleadingly at my forceful partner. There was no reprieve in his dark brown eyes. Reaching the end of the counter, I cautiously looked up, the sounds of that falling chopper making my body judder with every blow. I made a dash for the corner and squatted, squeezing my bowels to make something happen. We were lucky it was still early morning and there were no customers to complicate things. After a few strained grunts, I began to have some success. Unfortunately, I'd forgotten to draw attention to myself and could have squatted there in peace for quite a long while had not Rumbo lost patience and begun yapping at me.

The butcher stayed his small meat chopper in mid-air and looked over to the doorway.

'Oh, it's you again, is it? Wait till I get hold of you,' he threatened.

He hastily placed his chopper on the counter and started making his way round towards Rumbo. That's when he saw me.

Our eyes met, his wide and disbelieving, mine wide and knowing only too well what was going to happen next.

'Oiii!' he cried, and his journey round the counter took on a new pace. I half rose, but running was a problem at that particular moment. Instead, I did a sort of undignified shuffling waddle towards the open doorway. Rumbo was already up at the counter, sorting out the nicest cut for himself while the butcher's whole attention was focused on me. The red-faced butcher had picked up a broom in the course of his journey, one of those heavy jobs used for scrubbing floors as well as sweeping. He waved it in the air before him like a knight's lance, its base aimed at my backside. There was no avoiding it and my awkward predicament didn't help matters.

Thank God the broom had a multitude of bristles, strong and hard but not as strong and hard as the handle would have been. I yelped as they cracked down on my rump, the butcher extending his arm so I was sent scuttling across the floor. I skidded and rolled but was up like a rabbit, running for the open doorway, Rumbo close on my heels, at least a pound and a half of raw steak hanging from his jaws.

'Oiiiii!' was all I heard from the butcher as I flew down the street, my partner-in-crime keeping pace and chuckling at his own cleverness.

Men and women hastily stepped to one side when they saw us coming and one man foolishly tried to snatch the dangling meat from Rumbo's mouth. Rumbo was too wily for that and easily avoided the grasping hand, leaving the man sprawled on hands and knees behind him. We ran on, Rumbo keeping a measured pace beside me and much amused by my panic. Finally he called out through his clenched mouth, 'This way, squirt, into the park!'

The urge to go my own way, to get away from this thief, was great, but my appetite was greater; besides, I'd earned my share of the booty. I followed him through rusted iron gates into what seemed to me to be acres and acres of lush greenery surrounded by giant foliage, but what must actually have been a fairly small city park. Rumbo disappeared into a clump of bushes and I chased after him, flopping into a panting, eyes-rolling heap on the soft soil two feet away from the spot where he'd decided to go to earth. He looked at me in a smirky way as I heaved in great lungfuls of air, nodding his head at some inner satisfaction. 'You did all right, pup,' he said. 'With a little bit of guidance you could amount to something. You're not like the other stupid dogs.'

I didn't need to be told that, but his praise pleased me all the same. Nevertheless, I growled at him. 'I could have been hurt there. I can't run as fast as you.'

'A dog can always outrun a man. He'd never have caught you.'

'He did, though,' I retorted, wriggling my rump to make sure nothing had been seriously damaged.

Rumbo grinned, 'You'll learn to take more than that in this life, pup. Men are funny creatures.' He turned his attention to the meat lying between his front paws, nudging it with his nose then licking the juices on it. 'Come on, come and get your share.'

I rose to my feet and gave my body a shake. 'I've got some unfinished business first,' I said huffily, and slunk off further into the bushes. When I returned only a few moments later, Rumbo was well into the raw steak, chomping and sucking in a disgusting manner. I hurried forward lest he swallowed the lot and launched myself into the meat in an equally disgusting manner. It was a fine meal, the finest I'd had since being a dog. Perhaps the excitement of the chase, the tension of the robbery, had increased my appetite, for even Bella's sausages hadn't tasted as good.

We lay among the bushes smacking our lips with satisfaction, our mouths still full of the steak's juicy blood flavours. After a while, I turned to my new companion and asked him if he often stole food in that way.

'Steal? What's steal? A dog has to eat to live, so you take food where you find it. You can't rely on what man gives you – you'd starve if you did – so you're on the lookout all the time, ready to grab anything that comes your way.'

'Yes, but we actually went into that butcher's and stole that meat,' I insisted.

'There's no such thing as steal for us. We're only animals, you know.' He looked at me meaningfully.

I shrugged my shoulders, unwilling or too content for the moment to pursue the matter further. But all the same I wondered just how aware Rumbo was.

He suddenly jumped to his feet. 'Come on, pup, let's play!' he shouted, and was gone, streaking through the bushes out on to the open grassland. A burst of energy swept through me as though a switch had been turned on somewhere inside, and I dashed after the older dog, yapping joyfully, tail erect, eyes gleaming. We chased, we rolled, we wrestled, Rumbo teasing me mercilessly, showing off his skills of speed, manoeuvrability and strength, submitting to my wilder onslaughts and tossing me aside with the slightest shrug just when I began to feel his equal. I loved it.

The grass was wonderful to wallow in, to rub our backs against, to breathe in its heady fumes. I'd have been happy to have stayed there all day, but after ten minutes or so a surly park-keeper came and chased us away. We mocked him at first, taunting him by coming within easy reach then dodging just as he took a swipe at us. Rumbo was the more daring, actually leaping up and giving the man a gentle push in the back when his attention was on me. The park-keeper's angry curses made us roar with laughter, but Rumbo soon tired of the game and was off through the gates without a word, leaving me to chase after him.

'Wait for me, Rumbo!' I called out, and he slowed his pace to a trot, allowing me to draw alongside.

'Where are we going *now*?' I asked.

'We're going to have our breakfast now,' he replied.

Rumbo led me through a confusing number of side-streets until we reached an enormous corrugated-iron wall running the length of the pavement. We reached a break in it and Rumbo trotted through, his nose twitching for some familiar scent.

'Good,' he said to me. 'He's in his office. Now listen to me, pup: stay good and quiet. The Guvnor doesn't have much patience with dogs, so don't be a nuisance. If he talks to you, just wag your tail and play dumb. Don't get frisky. If he's in a bad mood – I'll give you the nod if he is – make yourself scarce. We can try again later. O.K.?'

I nodded, beginning to feel apprehensive about meeting this 'Guvnor'. Looking around, I saw we were in a vast yard filled with old broken-up and broken-down cars, all piled in precarious-looking heaps. Other, smaller heaps, were scattered around and I saw these were made up of rusted parts from the damaged cars. A weary-looking crane stood at one end and I realised we were in a breaker's yard.

Rumbo had made his way towards a dilapidated wooden hut which stood in the centre of the metal-torn domain and stood scratching at its door, occasionally giving out a moderate bark. The shiny blue Rover parked near the hut stood out like a sore thumb among the mangled wrecks around it, the bright morning sun making its bodywork gleam disdainfully.

The door of the hut swung open and the Guvnor stepped out. ''Allo Rumbo, boy!' He beamed down at my tail-wagging friend; his mood seemed good. 'You been out all night again? You're supposed to be a guard dog, you know, stop me having headaches.' He squatted in front of Rumbo and ruffled the dog's fur, slapping his flanks for extra welcome, Rumbo was good – very good; he wagged his tail and shuffled his feet, grinning up at the Guvnor all the time, but not trying to thrust himself on to him, his tongue hanging loose, occasionally flicking upwards to lick the man's face. The Guvnor was heavily built, his long leather jacket bulging tight around the shoulders. He had that fleshy-looking hardness about him, a tough nut who had become used to the good things in life – good food and good liquor. A fat cigar protruded from his mouth and it looked a part of him, like his flattened nose; he would have looked silly without either. His hair, which was just beginning to thin, covered his ears and flowed over his collar at the back. A gold-sovereign ring flaunted itself from one hand while a large diamond ring outdid it on the other. He was about fortyish and had 'Villain' written all over him.

'Who's this you got with you?' The Guvnor looked over at me, surprise on his face. 'Got a little girl friend, have you?'

I bridled at his silly mistake. Fortunately, he corrected himself. 'Oh no, I can see he's just a pal. Here boy, come on.' He extended a hand towards me but I backed away, a little afraid of him.

'Get over here, squirt,' said Rumbo quietly, warning me with annoyance in his voice.

I crept forward cautiously, very uncertain of this man, for

59

he was a strange mixture of kindness and cruelty. Generally, when you taste them, people have both these qualities but usually one is more dominant than the other. With the Guvnor, both characteristics were equally balanced, something I now know is very common in men of his kind. I licked his fingers, ready to bolt at the least sign of aggression. He stopped me as I got carried away with his delicious flavours by clamping my jaws together with a big fist.

'What's your name then, eh?' He yanked at my collar and I tried to pull away, very fearful of him now.

'It's all right, squirt, he won't hurt you if you behave yourself,' Rumbo reassured me.

'No name? No address? Someone didn't want you very much, did they?' The Guvnor let me go, giving me a playful shove towards Rumbo. He stood up and I could sense I was instantly forgotten.

'O.K., Rumbo, let's see what the missis has sent you.' The man walked round to the boot of his Rover, unlocked it and pulled out an interesting-looking plastic bag – interesting because it bulged with what our noses told us could only be food. We danced around his ankles and he held the bag aloft out of reach. 'All right, all right, take it easy. Anyone would think you hadn't eaten for a week.' Rumbo grinned at me.

The Guvnor walked round to the back of the hut to where an old plastic bowl lay and emptied the contents of the bag into it. A meaty bone, soggy cornflakes, bits of bacon fat and half a chocolate bar fell into the bowl, a rich concoction of leftovers. There were even some cold baked beans among the scraps. As a human, my stomach would have turned over; as a dog, it was a gastronomic delight. Our noses disappeared into the mixture and for a few moments our minds were concentrated solely on filling our bellies. Rumbo got the tastier morsels, of course, but I didn't do too badly.

When the bowl was spotlessly clean, my friend wandered over to another bowl which stood beneath a dripping tap. He began to lap greedily at the water and I, my stomach fit to burst, drifted over and did the same. We slumped on the ground after that, too full to move.

'Do you eat this well every day, Rumbo?' I asked.

'No, not always. It's been a good morning. The Guvnor doesn't always bring me something – there've been times he hasn't fed me for days – and it's not always easy to steal. The shopkeepers around here are a bit wary of me now.'

The Guvnor had disappeared inside the hut and I could hear music blaring from a radio.

'Have you always belonged to the Guvnor?'

'I can't remember, to tell you the truth. He's all I've known.' Rumbo became deep in thought. Finally he said, 'No, it's no good. My mind goes fuzzy when I try to think too hard. Sometimes I remember scents when I sniff certain people. They seem familiar to me. I can't remember not knowing the Guvnor, though. He's always been there.'

'Is he good to you?'

'Most of the time. Sometimes he ties me up when he wants to make sure I stay in all night, and sometimes he kicks me hard for shouting too loudly. But I can't help it. He's got some nasty friends and I just let fly at them when they come round.'

'What do they do here?'

'Talk mostly. They stay in that hut for hours, arguing and laughing. There's a few regulars who do the work around here, mess around with those heaps of junk, and things; bring new ones in. They're never very busy.'

'What does the Guvnor do?'

'You're a bit nosy aren't you, squirt?'

'Sorry. I'm just interested, that's all.'

Rumbo eyed me suspiciously for a few moments. 'You're not like other dogs, are you? You're . . . Well, you're a bit like me. Most dogs are very stupid. You're stupid, but not in the same way. Where exactly *are* you from, pup?'

I told him all I could remember and discovered I was beginning to forget my past also. I could still remember the market where I was bought, but not much more between there and the dogs' home. It's something that's happening to me more and more; I have periods of complete lucidity, then my mind can go virtually blank – my past, my origins, a vague blur. I often forget I was a man.

I didn't voice my anxiety over my human ancestry at that time because I didn't want to alarm Rumbo in any way; I needed him so I could learn how to survive as a dog. Acceptance of circumstances comes more easily to an animal, you see, and it was that animal part of me which turned away maddening thoughts.

'You were lucky to get away from the dogs' home, pup. That's the death-house for many,' Rumbo said.

'Have you ever been inside?'

'No, not me. They'll never catch me as long as I can run.'

'Rumbo, why aren't all dogs like us? I mean, why don't they talk like us, think like us?'

He shrugged. 'They just aren't.'

'Rumbo, were you ever . . . do you ever remember being . . . er, have you always been a dog?'

His head jerked up. 'What are you talking about? Of course I've always been a dog? What else could I have been?'

'Oh, nothing.' My head sank miserably down on to my paws. 'I just wondered.'

'You're a strange pup. Don't cause me any trouble here, shrimp, otherwise I'll turn you out. And stop asking silly questions.'

'Sorry, Rumbo,' I said and quickly changed the subject. 'What does the Guvnor do?' I asked again.

Rumbo's answering glare and bared teeth killed my curiosity for the moment. I decided to take a little nap, but just before I dozed off another thought struck me.

'Why don't men understand us when we talk, Rumbo?'

His voice was drowsy with sleep when he replied. 'I don't know. Sometimes the Guvnor understands me when I talk to him, but usually he just ignores me, tells me to quit yapping. Humans are just as stupid as stupid dogs sometimes. Now leave me alone, I'm tired.'

It was then that I realised we hadn't actually been communicating with words: it had been our *minds* speaking to each other. All animals or insects – fish even – have a way of communication whether it's by sound, scent or body display, and I've come to learn that even the dumbest creature has some sort of mental link with his own species – as well as others. It goes far beyond physical communications: how do you explain individual grasshoppers grouping into a swarm of locusts, what makes soldier ants march, what suddenly makes the lemming decide it's time to jump in the sea? Instinct, communication by body secretions, the sense of race survival: they all play their part, but it goes deeper. I'm a dog, and I know.

But I didn't know then. I was a pup, and a confused one at that. I'd found a friend I could talk to through my mind, someone who was more like me than the other dogs I'd met; few had come close, but none were like old Rumbo. I gazed at him fondly through blurred eyes, then I dozed off.

Eight

They were good, those days with Rumbo. The first morning had been enlightening and the days that followed were an education. We spent a large part of the time foraging for food, visiting the huge market most mornings (it slowly dawned on me that this was Nine Elms, the fruit and veg. market which had been yanked cruelly from the Covent Garden area to an obscure South Thames position, so I knew I was in South London, somewhere around Vauxhall) and then visiting the shops to see what we could steal. I soon learned to be as swift and cunning as Rumbo, but I never became as audacious. He would disappear into an open doorway of a house and seconds later calmly stroll out with a packet of biscuits, or a loaf, or anything he could lay his jaws on (he once emerged with a leg of lamb between his teeth but he didn't get away with that; a coloured lady came flying out and frightened old Rumbo so much with her shrieking he dropped the meat and bolted, a thrown milk bottle shattering on the pavement behind him).

Once we came across one of those pastry vans unloading its morning delivery. It was filled with trays of sweet-smelling buns and cakes, not to mention freshly baked bread. Rumbo waited until the driver had taken a large tray of pastries into the baker's, then leapt into the open interior of the van. I held back, of course, coward that I am, and watched enviously as Rumbo jumped from the van with a lovely sugared bun glued to his mouth. He crouched beneath the vehicle wolfing his booty as the driver returned for another tray. When he went back into the shop, freshly laden, Rumbo was up inside the van again, gulping down the remains of the first bun while snatching a chocolate éclair from another tray. He did this three times, each time hiding beneath the van before the driver returned, swallowing as fast as he could, when the dope (me) decided to chance his arm. I waited until the man was well inside the shop, scrambled up into the van (no easy task for a pup) and fussily sniffed my way along the delicious racks of confectionery. Rumbo was in and out like a shot, needless to say, but me – I had to be choosy. I had just decided upon a large, succulent-looking lemon meringue tart, torn between it and the chocolate éclair oozing cream lying beside it, when a shadow fell across the open doorway.

I yelped in fright and the man yelped in surprise. His surprise turned to menace and my fright turned to more fright. I tried to explain I was starving, that I hadn't eaten for a week, but he wasn't having any of it. He lurched forward and grabbed for my collar; I backed further into the van. The man cursed and hauled himself inside, crouching so he wouldn't hit his head on the low roof. He advanced on me and I retreated as far as I could go, which wasn't far enough. It's an unpleasant feeling when you know you're going to be hurt and, I must admit, I indulged in pity for myself to the full. Why had I allowed myself to be led on by that thief Rumbo, that crook in dog's clothing? Why had I let myself be bullied into this low life of petty thieving by this sneaky mongrel?

And then there he was, good old Rumbo, on the tail-end of the van, snarling at the delivery man's back, shouting defiantly at him. He was magnificent! The man turned in alarm, bumped his head on the roof, lost his balance and fell backwards on to the trays with their squashy contents. He slipped almost to the floor of the van, only the confined space saving him, and his elbows sunk into the creamy goodies behind him.

I dodged over his sprawled legs and leapt from the van, running even as I landed. Rumbo took his time and helped himself to one more delicacy before he jumped down after me. When we stopped, about a hundred miles later, he was smacking his lips contentedly. I panted my thanks to him and he grinned in his superior way. 'Sometimes, squirt, you're as dumb as the other mutts – maybe dumber. Still, I suppose it takes time to teach a new dog old tricks.' For some reason, he thought that was very funny and repeated it to himself over and over for the rest of that day.

Another trick of Rumbo's, using me as bait, was his diversion tactic. I would gallop up to an unsuspecting, shopping-bag-laden housewife and use all my puppy charms to make her lower her burden to the ground and pet me, maybe even offer me a titbit. If she had children with her it was even easier, for she would be forced into making a fuss of me with them, or at least drag them away. When all her attention was on me – I'd be licking her face or rolling on the ground, offering my tummy to be rubbed – Rumbo would rummage through her unguarded shopping. When he found something tasty he would streak off, leaving me to make my excuses and follow at a more leisurely pace. We often got found out before he'd grabbed anything useful, but that didn't spoil the enjoyment of the game.

Taking sweets from babies was another delightful pastime. Mothers would howl and their offspring would bawl as we scooted off with our prizes. Sudden raids on kids around ice-cream vans were always rewarding, the van's jangling jingle acting as a homing beacon for us. The coming of winter, forced us to cut down on this kind of activity unfortunately, for the parks were empty and the ice-cream vans in hibernation.

Rumbo loved to taunt other dogs. He looked down on all other animals as inferiors, resenting their stupidity, especially dogs, most of whom he considered more feeble-minded than any other living creature. I don't know why he held such a prejudice against dogs; it may have been because he was ashamed of them, ashamed they didn't have his intelligence, his dignity. Oh yes, rogue that he was, Rumbo had lots of dignity. Rumbo never begged, for instance; he asked for food, or he stole it, but he never grovelled for it. Sometimes he might act out a parody of a dog begging for food or affection, but this was always for his own cynical amusement. He taught me that life took advantage of the living, and to exist – really to *exist* – you had to take advantage of life. In his opinion, dogs had let themselves become slaves to man. *He* wasn't owned by the Guvnor, he did a job of work for him by guarding the yard, thereby earning his keep, such as it was. The Guvnor understood this and their relationship was based on mutual respect. I wasn't sure the Guvnor had such finer feelings, but I kept my opinion to myself, for I was only a pupil – Rumbo was the master.

Anyway, my companion never lost a chance of telling another dog how stupid he was. Poodles were his greatest source of derision and he would laugh uncontrollably at their clipped curls. The poor old dachshund came in for a bellyful too. Rumbo didn't care whom he picked on, be it an Alsatian or a Chihuahua. However, I did once witness him go very quiet and reflective when a Dobermann passed us by.

He got himself, and often me, into some fine old scrapes, other dogs sensing our difference and ganging up on us. I suffered as a pup, but it certainly toughened me up. I learned to run a lot faster too. The funny thing was, Rumbo could have been leader of the pack easily, for he was strong as well as smart, a good combination for the dog world; but he was essentially a loner, he went where he wanted to go, unhampered by thoughts of others. I'm still not sure why he took up with me; I can only suppose he recognised our mutual freakishness.

He was a Romeo, too. He loved the ladies, did Rumbo, and there again, size or breed meant nothing to him. He would disappear for days, returning with a tired but smug grin on his face. When I asked where he'd been, he always said he'd tell me when I was old enough to know.

I always knew when he would be off, for a strangely exciting smell would suddenly fill the air and Rumbo would stiffen, sniff, and bolt out of the yard – with me vainly trying to follow. It would be a bitch in heat of course, somewhere in the neighbourhood, possibly a couple of miles away, but I was too young to know about such things. So I'd wait patiently for his return, moping around until he did, angry at being left behind. Still, Rumbo was always pretty easy to live with for the next few days.

Another great pastime of his was rat-catching. God, how he hated rats, that Rumbo! There were never many in the yard, he made sure of that, but occasionally the odd two or three would make a reconnoitre, looking for a fresh supply of food, I suppose, or perhaps a new breeding ground. Rumbo would always know when they were about, he had a sixth sense for it. His hairs would bristle and his lips curl back revealing yellow fan-like teeth, and he'd snarl a deep menacing animal snarl. It would frighten the life out of me. Then he'd creep forward, taking his time, and he'd mooch through the old junks, oblivious of me, a hunter stalking his prey, a killer closing in on his kill. At first, I'd stay in the background, the vile creatures terrifying me with their evil looks and their foul language, but eventually Rumbo's hate passed on to me, turning my fear into revulsion then detestation. Detestation led to anger, and anger overcame my nervousness. So we'd rout the rats together.

Mind you, they were brave, some of those rats, loathsome as they were. The sight of nice juicy puppy flesh may have had something to do with their fearlessness, and in those early days my life was often in jeopardy, and it's thanks to Rumbo that I'm still in one piece today. (Of course, he soon realised what wonderful rat-bait he possessed, and it wasn't long before he'd coaxed me into acting as such.) As the months went on, my meat became more stringy – thin I think you'd call me, despite our scavenging – and my legs longer, my jaws and teeth stronger. The rats no longer regarded me as dinner but as diner and treated me with much more respect.

We never really ate them. We'd tear them to pieces, we'd break their bones – but their flesh just wasn't to our taste, no matter how hungry we felt at the time.

Rumbo loved to taunt them when he had them cornered. They'd hiss and curse at him, threaten him, bare their cruel teeth, but he would only sneer, taunt them all the more. He would advance slowly, his eyes never leaving theirs, and the rats would back away, bunch up their hindquarters, their bodies tensed for the leap forward. They'd make their move and Rumbo would make his. Dog and rat would meet in mid-air and the ensuing fight would be almost too frenzied to follow with the eye. The outcome was always inevitable: a high-pitched squeal, a stiff-haired body flying through the air, and Rumbo pouncing triumphantly on his broken-necked opponent as it landed in a nerve-twitching heap. Meanwhile, I was left to deal with any of the unfortunate vermin's companions, and this I learned to do almost as ably – but never with quite as much relish – as Rumbo.

We almost came unstuck one day, however.

It was winter, and the mud in the yard was frost-hard. The yard itself was locked and deserted – it must have been a Sunday – and Rumbo and I were warm and snug on the back seat of a wrecked Morris 1100 which was acting as a sort of temporary bedsitter until more suitable accommodation came along (our previous lodgings, a spacious Zephyr, having been broken up completely and sold as scrap). Rumbo's head shot up first and mine was a close second; we'd heard a noise and that familiar rank smell was in the air. We crept silently from the battered car and followed our noses towards the odour's source, in among the jumble of wrecks, through the narrow alleyways of twisted metal, the rat scent drawing us on, the occasional scratching against metal making our ears twitch. We soon came upon them.

Or rather, he came upon us.

We had stopped before a turn in the path through the cars, aware that our prey lay just around the corner, the strong smell and the scratching noises our informant, and were tensing up for the rush when, suddenly he appeared before us.

He was the biggest rat I'd ever seen, more than half my size (and I'd grown considerably), his hair was brown and his incisors were long and wicked-looking. The creature was just as startled as us by the sudden confrontation and disappeared instantly, leaving us to blink our eyes in surprise. We rushed round the corner, but he was gone.

'Looking for me?' came a voice from somewhere high up. We looked around us in bewilderment then spotted the rat together. He was perched on the roof of a car and looking down at us contemptuously.

'Up here, you mangy-looking curs. Coming up to get me?' he said.

Now rats aren't generally given much to conversation, most of them just spit and swear or scowl a lot, but this was the talkingest rat I'd ever come across.

'I've heard about you two,' he went on. 'You've caused us a lot of problems. At least, so the ones who've managed to get away tell me.' (You can't catch 'em all.) I've been wanting to meet you both – especially you, the big one. Think you're a match for me?'

I had to admire Rumbo's nerve, for I was set to run and hide. The rat may have been smaller than me, but those teeth and claws looked as though they could do a lot of damage to tender dog-meat. However, Rumbo spoke up, not a trace of nervousness in his voice: 'Are you going to come down, mouth, or do I have to come up and get you?'

The rat actually laughed – rats don't laugh much – and settled himself into a more comfortable position. 'I'll come down, cur, but in my own time; first I want to talk.' (*Certainly* no ordinary rat this.) 'What exactly have you got against us rats, friend? I know we're loved neither by man nor animal, but you have a special dislike, haven't you? Is it because we're scavengers? But then aren't you worse? Aren't all captured animals the lowest scavengers because they live off man – as parasites? Of course, you can't even dignify your existence with the word "captured" because most of you choose that way of life, don't you? Do *you* hate us because we're free, not domesticated, not . . . ' he paused, grinning slyly, ' . . . neutered as you are?'

Rumbo bridled at this last remark. 'I'm not neutered, rat-face, they'll never do that to me!'

'It doesn't have to be a physical thing, you know,' the rat said smugly. 'It's your mind I'm talking about.'

'I've still got a mind of my own.'

'Have you, have you?' The rat snorted. 'At least we vermin run free, no keepers for us.'

'Who the hell would want you?' Rumbo scoffed. 'You even turn on each other when things get rough.'

'That's called survival, dog. Survival.' The rat was displeased. He rose to his feet. '*You* hate us because you know we're all the same – man, animal, insect – all the same, and *you* know rats live an existence others try to hide. Isn't that so, dog?'

'No, it's not so, and *you* know that!'

There were a lot of 'you knows' flying around. Unfortunately, *I* didn't know what they were talking about.

Rumbo advanced towards the car, his coat bristling with rage.

'There's a reason for rats living the way they do, just as there's a reason for the way dogs live. And you know it!'

'Yes, and there's a reason for me to tear your throat out,' the rat spat at Rumbo.

'That'll be the day, ratface!'

They ranted at each other for another five minutes before their anger finally boiled over. And it boiled over in a strange way.

Both rat and dog went suddenly quiet as though there were nothing left to say. They glared into each other's eyes, Rumbo's brown and bulging, the rat's yellow and evil; both pairs were filled with hate. The tension between them mounted, a screaming silence, a building of venom. Then, with a squeal, the rat launched himself from the car roof.

Rumbo was ready. He leapt aside so that the vermin landed heavily on the hard earth, then struck out for the rat's neck. But the rat squirmed away and turned to meet Rumbo's charge. Teeth clashed against teeth, and claws dug into flesh.

I stood there, stunned and fearful, watching them try to tear each other to pieces. Growls, snarls and squeals came from the struggling bodies, but it was Rumbo's yelp that set me into action. I rushed forward, shouting at the top of my bark, trying to find the rage to give me the courage. There wasn't much I could do, for they were locked together in a writhing embrace, rolling over and over, flaying each other with their feet, biting, drawing blood, ripping skin. I could only lunge in whenever I caught sight of that stinking brown fur, nipping at it with bared teeth.

Quite suddenly, they drew apart, panting, beaten, but still glaring into each other's eyes. I saw that Rumbo's shoulder was badly torn and one of the rat's ears was shredded. They crouched, bodies quivering, low growling sounds at the backs of their throats. I thought perhaps they were too exhausted to carry on, but then I realised they were only regathering their strength.

They sprang at each other again and this time I sprang with them. Rumbo caught the rat by the throat and I managed to bite into one of his front legs. The taste of warm blood sickened me, but I clung to the creature with all my strength. He rolled and squirmed and snapped at us; I felt a sharp pain across my shoulders as he scythed across them with his teeth. The shock made me lose my grip of his leg and, twisting his body, the rat kicked out at me with his hind legs, sending me rolling across the frozen mud.

I rushed straight in and received a deep gash across my nose from the rodent's claws. The pain sent me back again, but I returned just as quickly. Rumbo still had the rat by the throat, endeavouring to lift him from the ground and toss him, a trick I'd seen him use to break other vermin's backs. The rat was too big, though – too heavy. At least the grip Rumbo held prevented the rat doing serious damage with those teeth; he'd cut my shoulders but could have seriously wounded me had his incisors been allowed to sink in. Such was his strength that the big rat managed to break away. He ran free, turned, and streaked back into us, twisting his head from left to right, striking at our vulnerable bodies with his vicious weapons. Rumbo cried out as he was gored along the flank. He staggered to one side and the rat, with a shout of triumph, flew at him. But in his excitement, he'd forgotten about me.

I leapt on to the rat's back, bringing him down with my weight, and biting into the top of his head, breaking a tooth against his skull. The rest was messy and unglorious: Rumbo leapt back into the fray, and between us we managed to kill the creature. The rat didn't die easily, and even to this day I have a grudging admiration for the fight he put up against two heavier opponents. When his squirming finally stopped and the last gasp left his bloody body, I felt not just exhausted but degraded too. He had had just as much right to live as we had, despicable though he was in the eyes of others, and his courage could not be denied. I think Rumbo felt the same sense of shame even though he said nothing.

He dragged the dead body out of sight beneath a car (I don't know why – a sort of burial, I suppose) and returned to lick my wounds for me.

'You did well, pup,' he said wearily between licks. His voice had a quietness to it that was unusual for him. 'He was a big brute. Different from most I've met.'

I whimpered as his tongue flicked across the gash in my nose.

'What did he mean, Rumbo, when he said we're all the same?'

'He was wrong. We're not.'

And that was all my friend had to say on the subject.

The rat incident soured me for the killing of others of the species; I'd fight them certainly, chastise them, but from then on I let them escape. Rumbo soon became aware of my reluctance to kill and grew angry with me; he still hated the creatures and slew them whenever we came in contact with them, perhaps with less relish than before, but with a cold determination.

I've no wish to dwell on our dealings with vermin, for it was an unpleasant and ugly part of my dog life, albeit a very small part; but one other incident has to be mentioned because it shows just how deep Rumbo's hate went for these unfortunate and unblessed creatures.

We came across a nest of them. It was at the far end of the yard and in a car which lay at the very bottom of a tumble of others. The vehicle's roof was crushed flat, there were no doors, and nestled among the stuffing of a torn back seat were a dozen tiny pink rats suckling from their recumbent mother. Their little bodies were still glistening and slick from their birth. The scent drew us like a magnet and we wriggled our way through the twisted junk to reach them. When I saw the babies and the alarmed parent, I prepared to retreat, to leave them in peace. But not Rumbo. He tore into them with a fury I'd never seen before.

I called out to him, pleaded with him, but he was oblivious to my cries. I ran from the place, not wanting to witness such slaughter, and flew from the yard, away from that terrible destruction.

We didn't speak for days after that; I was bewildered by Rumbo's savagery and he was puzzled by my attitude. It has, in fact, taken me a long time to come to terms with the brutality of animal life, and of course it was my very 'humanness' which hindered my progress (or regress – however you care to look at it) towards this acceptance. I think Rumbo put my sulkiness down to growing pains, for growing I certainly was. My puppy fat had almost disappeared entirely, my legs were long and strong (although my back legs were a little cow-hocked). My toenails had been kept trimmed by the constant running on hard concrete and my teeth were firm and sharp. My vision was still excellent, still vivid, unusually lucid. (Rumbo had the normal dog's eyesight: not quite as good as man's and unable to distinguish colours too well. He could see all right in the dark, though, perhaps better than me.) My appetite was extremely healthy and I had no trouble with worms, tartar on the teeth, mange, constipation, diarrhoea, irritable bladder, eczema, ear-canker, nor any other normal dog ailments. Nevertheless I did itch a lot and it was this irritation that brought Rumbo and me together again.

I had observed him scratching with more and more frequency and, I had to admit, it had become almost a full-time occupation for me, this sucking of fur and raking of skin with hind legs. When I actually saw the little yellow monsters hopping freely over my companion's back like grasshoppers on a heath, my disgust for our condition forced me to make a comment.

'Doesn't the Guvnor ever bath us, Rumbo?'

Rumbo stopped his scratching and eyed me with surprise. 'Fleas annoying you, are they, squirt?'

'Annoying me? I feel like a walking hostel for parasites.'

Rumbo grinned. 'Well you won't like the Guvnor's method of dealing with it.'

I inquired what the method was.

'Whenever he gets fed up with my scratching or can't stand the smell any more, he ties me to a drainpipe, then turns a hose on me. I try to keep out of his way when I'm particularly rancid.'

I shivered at the thought. It was mid-winter.

'There's another way,' Rumbo went on. 'It's just as cold, but at least it's more effective.'

'Anything. Anything's better than this itching.'

'Well,' he hesitated, 'I usually reserve this for warmer times, but if you insist . . . '

I took up my usual position on his left, my head level with his flank, and we trotted out of the yard. He took me to a park, a big one this, and quite a distance from our home. The park contained a pond. And when we reached it, Rumbo told me to jump in.

'Are you kidding?' I said. 'We'll freeze to death. Besides, I don't even know if I can swim.'

'Don't be daft,' Rumbo retorted. 'All dogs can swim. As for the cold, you'll find this less unpleasant than being hosed down by the Guvnor. Come on, give it a try.'

With that he plunged into the water, much to the delight of the few children and their parents who were about that wintry morning. Rumbo paddled out to the middle of the pond, swift and confident. He even ducked his head beneath the surface, something I'd never seen a dog do before. I could just imagine the panic among those fleas as they fled to the top of his head, the last refuge on a sinking island, and then their dismay as even this sunk below the waters. He swam in an arc and headed back towards me, calling out for me to join in. But I was too much of a coward.

He reached the bank and hauled himself out. Mothers dragged their offspring away, for they knew what was going to happen next. The dope (yes, me) didn't.

I was drenched with a freezing shower of water as my friend (my crafty friend) shook his whole body to rid his fur of excess moisture. I felt foolish as well as angry; I'd seen dogs do this often enough in my past life, so I shouldn't have been caught napping. Anyway, there I stood, dripping wet, as cold as if I'd plunged in myself.

'Come on, squirt, you're wet enough. You might as well go the whole way now,' Rumbo laughed.

I shivered and had to admit he was right. There was no point in not going in now. I crept towards the edge of the pond and gingerly dipped in a front paw. I pulled it out fast; the water was colder than freezing! I turned my head to tell Rumbo I'd changed my mind, I could put up with the itching for a few more months till the weather got warmer. I barely caught a glimpse of his big black body as he hurtled himself at me. With a yelp of surprise, I fell head-first into the pond, Rumbo tumbling in behind.

I came up spluttering, gasping for air, my mouth and throat, my nose, my ears, my eyes filled with choking water.

'Ooh!' I cried. 'Ooooh!' And over the sound of my splashing I could hear Rumbo laughing. I wanted to strike back at him, I wanted to drown him, but I was too busy trying to survive the cruel pond. My teeth were chattering and my breathing came in short, desperate gasps. Pretty soon – when I realised I could swim – the unpleasantness drowned instead of me and I began to enjoy this new experience. I kicked out with my back legs and paddled with my paws, just managing to keep my nose above the waterline. The effort prevented my limbs from going completely numb and I found I could use my tail as a sort of rudder.

'How d'you like, pup?' I heard Rumbo call out.

Looking about, I saw that he was back in the centre of the pond. I made towards him.

'It's g-good, Rumbo, b-but it's cold,' I replied, my anger forgotten.

'Huh! You wait till you get out!' He submerged again and came up smiling. 'Down you go, pup, put your head under or you'll never get rid of them!'

I remembered the point of the exercise and ducked my head beneath the surface. I came up coughing.

'Again, pup, again! Go right under or they'll never leave you!'

Down I went again, this time holding my breath and staying under for as long as possible. I don't know what the people on the bank thought, for it must have been a peculiar sight to see two mongrels acting like performing seals. We romped around in the water, splashing and barging into each other, thoroughly cleansing ourselves with our vigorous actions. Five minutes was enough, and by mutual consent we headed for the shore. We clambered out, deliberately drenched the human onlookers, and began a game of chase to warm ourselves up.

By the time we got home we were both laughing and giggling, feeling fresh and alive as never before – and, of course, ravenous. We found a well-wrapped packet of sandwiches that one of the Guvnor's workmen had foolishly left lying on a bench while he dismantled a broken engine, and we took them to our snug bedsitter, scoffing the lot within seconds. For once, to my surprise, we shared the food equally, Rumbo making no attempt to gobble the major portion. He grinned at me as I finished the last few crumbs and, after smacking my lips contentedly, I grinned back at him. Our differences were forgotten and Rumbo and I were friends again. There was a subtle change, however: I wasn't exactly equal to Rumbo now, but I was a little less inferior than I had been.

The pupil was beginning to catch up with the master.

Nine

So what of my feelings of being a man in a dog's body?

Well, they certainly never left me, but they didn't often play an important part in my thinking. You see, I was developing as a *dog*, and this development took up most of my time. I was always conscious of my heritage and my human instincts often took over from my canine tendencies, but my physical capabilities were those of a dog (apart from my extraordinary vision) and this governed my attitude. There were many times – nights mostly – when memories fought their way to the surface and questions, questions, questions, tussled with my mind; and there were many times when I was completely and wholly a dog, with no other thoughts but dog thoughts.

I recognised my similarity to Rumbo and I'm sure he recognised it too. The disturbing fact was that I also recognised it in the big rat. Had Rumbo? He was deliberately vague when I tackled him on our difference to others of our kind, and I was never quite sure whether he understood it or if it was just as big a mystery to him. He would shrug his shoulders and dismiss the subject with a remark such as 'Some animals are dumber than others, that's all.' But I would often find him regarding me with a thoughtful look in his eyes.

So I lived my life with Rumbo and the urge to discover the truth of my existence was held in abeyance while I learned to live that life.

Like all dogs, I was fanatically curious; nothing near me went unsniffed, nothing loose went untugged, and nothing pliable went unchewed. Rumbo would lose patience, scold me for behaving like any other stupid mutt (although he liked a good sniff and chew himself) and would generally berate me for my inquisitiveness. We had many afternoons or evenings when he did answer my questions (he had to be in a relaxed and talkative mood to do so), but when he thought too long or too deeply he would become confused and irritable. I often seemed to be about to learn something of significance – perhaps a clue to my own strange existence or a reason for our obviously more advanced development to others of our kind – when his eyes would become blank and he'd go into a long, trance-like silence. It would frighten me, for I would think I'd pushed him too far, his searching mind becoming lost within itself, unable to find the route back. On such occasions I was afraid he'd become just another dog. Then he would blink a few times, look around curiously as though surprised at his surroundings, and carry on talking, ignoring the question I'd asked. These were strange and apprehensive moments for me, so I refrained from triggering them off too frequently.

Other apprehensive moments were when we saw ghosts. It didn't happen often enough for it to become a common occurrence, but enough to be disconcerting. They would drift sadly by, a feeling more than an expression of utter loneliness about them, and some seemed to be in a state of shock, as if they had been torn brutally from their earthly bodies. Rumbo and I would freeze at the sight, but we'd never bark as other dogs might. My companion would warn them to keep away from us with a low growling, but we were of no interest to these spirits and they would drift on without even acknowledging our presence. On one occasion – it was in broad daylight – four or five ghosts, bunched tightly together, wandered through the yard like a small, drifting cloud. Rumbo had no explanation for the phenomenon and forgot about it as soon as it had passed, but it puzzled me for a long time afterwards.

The comings and goings of more mortal beings into the yard began to increase. There were normally two or three full-time overalled men working in the yard, breaking up the junks, and a steady stream of customers looking for cheap parts. Gigantic lorries (gigantic to me) would be loaded with crushed car bodies by the yard's crane, then disappear through the gates with their valuable metal. Vehicles battered beyond repair or too old and tired to run anymore were brought in and dumped unceremoniously on top of precariously balanced scrap piles. But it was a different increase in activity that aroused my curiosity.

The Guvnor began to have frequent visitors who had no interest in the yard itself, but would disappear into his office and remain there for hours on end. They arrived in twos and threes and left in the same numbers. They came from different areas, mostly from Wandsworth and Kennington, but others from Stepney, Tooting, Clapham, with a few from nearby outlying counties. I knew this because I'd listened to their conversations as they waited outside the hut for the Guvnor's arrival (he was often late). One or two would even play with me, or torment me in a friendly way. Rumbo frowned upon my childishness with these men, for they never offered food nor were they relevant to our life-style (Rumbo was choosy about offering his friendship), but I, like any other pup, wanted to be loved by everyone and anyone. I didn't know what their business with the Guvnor was (I noticed they treated him with a lot of respect), nor did I care much; I was just curious because they were outsiders and I could learn more about the other places from them – not just the surrounding area, for I knew enough about that – but other parts further away. I was looking for clues, you see, clues about myself. I felt the more I discovered – or rediscovered – about the world outside, the more chance I had of solving my own riddle.

It was on one such occasion, in fact, that I earned my permanent name. Some of the workmen in the yard had taken to calling me Horace (God knows why, but it seemed to tickle them), and it was a name I detested. They used it in a mocking way and usually – unless they were offering something (which was rare) – I ignored their calls with a nose-up dignity. Even Rumbo, in moments of sarcasm, would call me Horace rather than 'squirt'. In the end, even I was beginning to get used to it.

However, the Guvnor had never bothered to give me a name – I was never important enough to him for that – and he really didn't have much cause to refer to me anyway after our initial meeting months before. I was grateful, at least, that he hadn't picked up this awful nickname from his workmen.

So this is how I got a proper and appropriate name.

A small group of the outsiders had gathered in front of the Guvnor's office – hut – and were awaiting his arrival. Rumbo was away on one of his 'bitch-in-season' jaunts and I was wandering aimlessly around the yard, sulking at being left behind again. I trotted over to the group to see if I could overhear anything of interest (or perhaps to beg for some affection). One of the younger men saw me coming and crouched low, a hand outstretched, to welcome me. 'Ere, boy. Come on.'

I bounced towards him, pleased to be called. 'What's your name, then, eh?'

I didn't want to tell him I was called Horace so I kept quiet and licked his hand.

'Let's 'ave a look at you,' he said, pulling my collar round with his other hand. 'No name on this, is there? Let's see what we've got for you.' He stood up, reaching into his overcoat pocket and my tail began to wag when he produced a small green tube of sweets. He levered a sweet out and held it up for me to see. I went up on my hind legs immediately, mouth gaping for the treat to be dropped into. The man laughed and let the little round sweet fall and I caught it deftly on my tongue, crunching and gulping it down by the time my front legs touched ground again. I jumped up and put my muddy paws against him, asking politely for another; they had a nice minty flavour to them. He was a bit annoyed at the mud on his coat and pushed me down again, brushing at the marks left with his hand. 'Oh no, if you want another one, you've got to earn it. 'Eeyar', catch it.' He threw the mint high into the air and I jumped up to meet it on its downward journey, catching it smartly. The young man laughed and his bored companions began to take an interest. They had been lounging against the car they'd arrived in, a maroon Granada, stamping their feet to keep the circulation flowing, their coat collars turned up against the cold.

'Let's see 'im do it again, Lenny,' one of them said.

The one called Lenny tossed another sweet and again I caught it in mid-air.

'Do it a bit 'igher next time.'

Lenny tossed and I jumped. Success once more.

'You're a clever old thing, aren't you?' said Lenny.

I had to agree; I was feeling quite pleased with myself. As Lenny poised a mint on his thumb and index finger I prepared to repeat my performance.

' 'Old on, Lenny.' A different man spoke this time. 'Make it do somethin' more difficult.'

'Like what?'

The group of men thought hard for a few moments, then one spotted a couple of tin mugs standing on the hut's windowsill. 'Use them,' he said, pointing towards the mugs. 'The old ball-an'-cones trick.'

'Do leave off! It's only a bleedin' dog, you know,' Lenny protested.

'Gorn, see if it can do it.'

He shrugged and walked over to the mugs. The regular yard workers used these for their tea-breaks, but I don't think they would have offered any objection to these men using them for other purposes. In fact, I had noticed that the Guvnor's regular employees kept well away from the business acquaintances of their boss. Lenny placed the two mugs upside-down on an even piece of ground while I nuzzled him for more sweets. He pushed me away and one of the men took hold of my collar to hold me back.

Lenny levered out a little round mint again and, in exaggerated motions, showed it to me, then placed it under one of the mugs. I pulled against the restraining hand, eager to get at the sweet.

Then Lenny did a puzzling thing: he placed a hand on either mug and whirled them in circles around each other, never letting their lips come off the ground. He did it slowly, but even so it was confusing for a mere dog. He stopped and nodded for the other man to let go. I bounded forward and immediately knocked over the mug which held the strong scent of mint.

I couldn't understand the group's cries of amazement and Lenny's delight as I gulped down the sweet. I accepted Lenny's friendly thumps on the back with a wagging tail, pleased that I had pleased him.

'Aah, it was a fluke. The dog couldn't do it again,' one of the men said. He was grinning though.

'Oh yes it could. It's a clever old thing, this pup,' Lenny retorted.

'Let's 'ave some money on it, then.'

The others agreed enthusiastically. It's funny what a group of bored men will find to amuse themselves.

Once again I was held back while Lenny went through his hand-holding-mint ballet. 'All right. A oncer says 'e does it again.' I was no longer an 'it' to Lenny.

'Right.'

'You're on.'

'Suits.'

And suddenly four pound notes appeared on the ground. The four men looked at me expectantly.

Lenny went through his mug swirling again and one of the men told him to speed it up. He did, and I must admit he had a definite flair for this sort of thing: the movements were baffling to the naked eye. But not to the sensitive nose. I had knocked over the mug and swallowed the sweet within three seconds of being released.

'Fantastic! 'E's a bloody marvel.' Lenny was delighted as he scooped up the four pounds.

'I still say it was a fluke,' a disgruntled voice muttered.

'Put your money where your mouth is, Ronald, my son.'

The bets were placed again, this time one of the men dropped out. 'He's sniffin' it out, I reckon,' he grumbled. This stopped the action; they hadn't thought of that.

'Nah,' Lenny said after a few moments' thought. ' 'E couldn't smell it with the mug over the top.'

'I dunno, it's pretty strong – peppermint.'

'O.K., O.K. Let's see what else we've got.'

The men rummaged through their pockets but came out with their hands empty. 'Just a minute,' one of them said and turned towards the Granada. He opened the driver's door, reached across the front seat and delved into the glove compartment. He came out with a half-eaten bar of chocolate. 'Keep it in there for the kids,' he said self-consciously. 'Keep the wrapper on so it don't smell so much.' He handed it to Lenny.

My mouth watered at the sight and I had to be firmly held back.

'Fair enough. Let's do it again.' Lenny made sure the wrapping covered all the exposed end of the chocolate and placed it careful beneath a mug. The mug had a nasty-looking grease smear on its base.

The fourth man rejoined the betting and, once more, Lenny's lightning hands went into action. Of course I made straight for the grease-smeared mug.

The chocolate was pulled from my mouth before it could be devoured, but Lenny was more generous with his praise. 'I could make a fortune with this dog,' he told the others, breaking off a tiny square of chocolate and popping it into my mouth. ''E's got brains, 'e's not as daft as 'e looks.' I bridled at this but the thought of more chocolate kept me sweet. ''Ow'd you like to come back to Edenbridge with me, eh? Connie and the kids'll love you. I could make a bomb out of some of the locals with you.'

'That's the Guv's dog, 'e won't let you 'ave it,' the one called Ronald said.

''E might. 'E's got two.'

'Anyway, I still say it was only luck. No dog's that clever.'

Lenny raised his eyes heavenwards. 'You wanna' see 'im do it again?'

Ronald was a bit more reluctant this time and the sound of a car pulling into the yard saved him from deciding whether to risk another pound or not. A sleek Jaguar stopped behind the Granada and the Guvnor stepped out; he changed his cars with more frequency than most people checked their tyres. He wore a heavy sheepskin coat and, of course, a fat cigar jutted comfortably from his mouth. The men greeted him with a friendliness born out of respect more than liking.

'What you lot up to?' He stuck his hands deep into his coat pockets as he swaggered his way round the Jag to the group.

'Just 'avin' a game with the dog 'ere, Guv,' said Lenny.

'Yeah, it's a clever little bugger,' said one of the others.

Lenny seemed hesitant to tell the Guvnor just how clever he

thought I was; plans for me were beginning to grow in his mind, I think.

'Nah, it could never do it again, never in a thousand years,' Ronald piped up.

'Do what, Ron?' the Guvnor asked affably.

'Lenny's done 'is ball-and-cones trick and the dog's guessed right every time,' another of the men said.

'Do me a favour!' the Guvnor scoffed.

'Nah, straight,' Lenny said, the thought of making some more instant cash overriding his future money-making plans.

'It must 'ave been a fluke. Dog's ain't that bright.'

'That's what I said, Guv,' Ronald chimed in.

'Yeah, and you lost your money, didn't you, my son,' Lenny grinned.

' 'Ow much you made so far, Lenny?'

' 'Er, let's see, Guv. Eight pounds in all.'

'All right. Eight more says it don't do it again.' He had style, the Guvnor.

Lenny hesitated for only a second. He chuckled and went down to the mugs again. 'Now then, boy, I'm relyin' on you. Don't let me down.' He looked at me meaningfully. For myself, I was enjoying the game; I liked pleasing this man, I liked him knowing I was no ordinary dog. I wasn't really grovelling for titbits. I was earning them.

Lenny shuffled the cups, even faster than before under the Guvnor's level gaze, but this time he'd placed the chocolate beneath the mug without the grease smear. He finished his intricate hand movements and looked up at the Guvnor. 'O.K.?' he asked.

The Guvnor nodded and Lenny looked across at me. 'O.K., boy, do your stuff.'

And at that moment Rumbo trotted into the yard.

Curiosity drew him over to the group, and when he saw me being held by the collar and the twin mugs set on the ground before me, he screwed up his brow in a puzzled frown. In an instant he had guessed a trick was being performed for the benefit of the men and I, his protégé, the mutt he had taken under his wing, the scruff in which he had tried to instil some dignity, was the star performer. Rising shame burnt my ears and I hung my head. I looked dolefully up at Rumbo, but he just stood there, his disgust apparent.

'Come on, boy,' Lenny urged. 'Get the chocolate. Come on!'

My tail drooped: I had let Rumbo down. He'd always taught me to be my own dog, never become a pet of man, never become inferior to them; and here I was, like some circus animal, performing tricks for their entertainment. I stepped towards the mugs, kicked the empty one over with a paw and trotted away in search of a dark hole in which to bury myself.

Lenny threw his hands up in the air in disgust and the Guvnor chuckled. Ronald, chortling loudly, stooped and picked up the Guvnor's winnings and handed them to him. As I disappeared round the corner of the hut, I heard the Guvnor say: 'I told you it was a fluke. Yeah – fluke. That's a good name for 'im. 'Ey, Georgie,' he called out to one of the yard workers. 'Get the pup's collar and put its name on it. Fluke! Yeah, that's good!' He was pleased with himself: the money meant nothing, but the scene had made him look good. He was making the most of it. I could still hear him chuckling as he unlocked the office door and the group of men disappeared through it.

So, I had a proper name. And like I say, it was appropriate: Fluke by name, fluke by nature.

Ten

Rumbo never mentioned that incident again. He was a little distant with me for a few days afterwards, but my final action had at least saved me some grace and, because of our need for each other (which Rumbo himself would never have admitted), we were soon back to our old relationship.

Lenny had lost interest in me, his plans for making money out of me dashed by my contrariness. Apart from a rueful grin now and again, he really didn't take much notice of me anymore when he came into the yard. The breaker called Georgie took my collar from me and returned it later. Rumbo told me there were scratch marks on the small metal nameplate and I assumed 'FLUKE' had been inscribed there. Anyway, that was what they called me in the yard now, and so did the people who petted me in the street once they'd looked at the collar. I was thankful I was no longer known as Horace.

The winter froze on and times for Rumbo and me got leaner. We still made our daily trips to the fruit-market, but our pickings in the shopping-zones had become increasingly more hazardous. The shopkeepers now knew us by sight and would chase us away as soon as we came sniffing around: the cold weather made the housewives more guarded, less friendly. I was fast losing my puppy cuteness (I suppose I was around seven or eight months old by then), and people are less inclined to stop and stroke a gangly mongrel than a plump, furry bundle, so I had become next to useless as a decoy for Rumbo. However, the hardship made us more cunning, swifter in our attacks, and more resourceful in our methods.

A wild dash through a supermarket usually proved fruitful,

provided there was a clear exit. One of us would knock stacks of cans over or generally cause a disturbance while the other would sneak in and grab the nearest edible item at hand. That was always very exciting. A romp around a school playground at lunchtime would inevitably yield a sandwich or two, or perhaps an apple or some chocolate. The pandemonium was lovely. A visit to the local street-market never failed to bring us replenishment for our greedy stomachs. The threats and curses our thieving from there caused was, nevertheless, a little alarming. Moreover, we had become too adventurous, and that led to our downfall.

One day Rumbo and I had marched boldly into a backyard, encouraged by our noses which had been enticed by delicious cooking smells. An open doorway stood before us and steam billowed out from within; we were at the back of a restaurant, at the kitchen entry. Both of us were over-confident to the point of recklessness; we had been getting away with it for too long. We ambled in.

It was a high-class restaurant, although you might never have suspected it from the state of the kitchen. I knew it was a good place because of the menu, part of which I could see steaming away on a centre table: roast duckling dripping with orange sauce. It was surrounded by other dishes, but not as mouth-watering, waiting to be carried away into the dining-room (or carried away by two hungry dogs). Apart from the chef, who had his stout back turned to us while he was busy stirring a huge cauldron of simmering soup, the kitchen was empty. Rumbo gave me a quick look, then with one bound was up on the table. I rested my front paws against the table's edge and smiled smugly. Our bellies would be full today.

Rumbo nonchalantly worked his way through the various dishes (if he had been a man, he'd have been humming) until finally he reached the duckling. He flicked out his tongue and began licking at the orange sauce. He looked back at me and I swear he rolled his eyes. My mouth was drooling by now and I was hopping from one hind foot to the other in frustration. Rumbo had a few more licks, then his jaws opened wide to grasp the entire roasted bird between them. It was at that moment the door leading to the dining-room burst open.

We stood paralysed as a waiter in a white jacket and small black bow-tie, carrying a tray full of half-empty dishes, breezed in, calling out a new order to the chef before he was even through the door. The waiter was fairly small for a man (all tall to me, you see) and wore his jet-black hair greasily slicked down. Above his greasily slicked down moustache was a long, curving nose and, above that, two over-large, bulbous eyes which grew even larger and more bulbous when he saw us. His mouth dropped open to a point where it almost matched Rumbo's and the dishes on his tray slid down the incline he had unconsciously created, slipping over the edge in an avalanche. The terrible crash as they hit the tiled floor set the whole scene in motion again.

The chef whirled, clutching at his heart, the waiter screamed, (I think he was Italian), Rumbo grabbed the duckling, and I (what else?), wet myself.

Rumbo leapt from the table, slid on a slippery patch on the floor, lost the duckling, scrambled to retrieve it, yelped as the hot soup-ladle thrown by the chef skimmed across his back, grabbed the duckling again by the parson's nose end, and scurried for the exit.

The waiter threw the now empty tray at Rumbo, choked back a sob, gave chase, skidded on the same slippery patch, sprawled on his back, and managed to get his legs tangled up in dog and duckling.

The chef moved his hand from his heart to his mouth, roared with furious anguish, lumbered forward, slid on the tray which covered another slippery patch left by the skidding orange-sauce-covered duckling, landed heavily (he was very stout) on the little waiter's chest, and bellowed and kicked at dog, duckling, waiter and all.

I ran away.

Rumbo crept furtively into the yard about five minutes after I'd arrived there. He crawled through our own private entrance at the back of the yard behind a huge pile of wrecks – a one-foot high hole torn in the corrugated-iron fencing at its base – still grasping the now cold roast duckling between his jaws. The young bird looked a bit worse for wear: a *pièce de résistance* that hadn't resisted too well. Nevertheless, to two hungry mongrels it was still a gastronomic triumph, and after we'd sucked every bone clean (I warned Rumbo not to crunch the bones – too splintery, I told him) we had a good chortle over our success. The smirks were wiped from our faces a couple of days later, however.

A uniformed policeman arrived at the yard and asked one of the breakers if there were two black mongrel dogs on the premises. Rumbo and I edged out of sight behind a decaying Ford Anglia and looked at each other nervously. It was obvious the shop-keepers had got together and registered a complaint to the local cop-shop; perhaps the restauranteur had instigated the action. It certainly hadn't taken the police long to track us down. We peeped from behind the old car and saw the breaker pointing nervously towards the Guvnor's office. The young policeman strolled casually over to the hut, examining the various cars parked alongside it. The Guvnor was having one of his now regular meetings with his cronies.

The plod knocked at the door and the Guvnor appeared. We watched his smiling face as he dealt with the policeman's inquiries, showing a disarming charm that had never been apparent to us before. His hands made gestures of surprise, alarm and concern; he nodded his head gravely, then shook it equally as gravely. Then he was back to smiling and smarming, his cigar never once leaving the corner of his mouth during the discourse. With one last smile of assurance from the Guvnor, the young policeman turned and strolled from the yard.

The Guvnor smiled benevolently at the policeman's back until he had disappeared through the gate: then he turned his gaze towards the rest of the yard, a look of sheer thunder on those now rock-like features. He spotted our snouts protruding from the wreck and marched towards us with stiff, determined strides.

'Run, squirt, run!' Rumbo warned me.

I wasn't quick enough. The Guvnor grabbed me before I had a chance to make a break for it. He began to flail at me with a closed fist, keeping a firm grip on my collar as he did so. I'd always felt the Guvnor had a contained cruelty about him (this didn't necessarily make him a cruel man) and now it was let loose and I was its recipient. I howled in pain, and was grateful that a dog's sensitive cells are unevenly distributed over the body otherwise some of these blows would have hurt even more.

Rumbo stood and watched from a distance, anxious for me and fearful for himself.

'Come 'ere, you!' the Guvnor bellowed, but Rumbo wasn't having any. He darted even further away. 'You wait 'till I get 'old of you,' my assailant shouted. Rumbo skipped from the yard.

The Guvnor's anger had been flushed now, but his meanness still remained. He dragged me to the back of the yard, collecting a length of rope on the way, then tied me to a wreck wedged beneath a pile of other wrecks.

'Right,' he snarled as he looped the rope around the empty window-frame of the car. 'Right!' He gave me one last wallop before he marched off, muttering something about the last thing he needed was the law snooping round. 'Right,' I heard him say as he slammed the hut door shut.

A few minutes later the door opened again and the Guvnor's cronies filed out, climbed into their various cars and drove off. After they'd gone the Guvnor appeared, roared for Rumbo and, when nothing happened went back inside. I had the feeling we wouldn't see old Rumbo for some time.

I tugged and pulled the rope, calling for the Guvnor to come back and let me loose; it was no use, he wouldn't listen. I was frightened to pull on the rope too hard because the cars towering above me looked precariously balanced; I could never figure out how the piles of cars in the yard never toppled. My calls turned into angry shouts, then piteous whining, then sorrowful whimpers and finally, much later on when the yard was deserted, sullen silence.

It was dark when my companion decided to return. I was shivering with the cold and miserable with the loneliness.

'I told you to run,' he said, coming out of the night.

I sniffed.

'He's got a terrible temper,' Rumbo went on, sniffing round me.

'Last time he tied me up, he left me for three days without any food.'

I looked at him reproachfully.

'Still, I can always bring you bits and pieces,' he added consolingly. Suddenly he looked up. 'Oh-oh. It's beginning to rain.'

A raindrop splattered against my nose.

'Not much cover here for you, is there?' he commented. 'Pity the car door's shut – you could've climbed in.'

I studied him quietly for a few moments, then looked away.

'Hungry?' he asked. 'I don't think I could find you anything this time of night.'

My head became dotted with rain-spots.

'Pity we ate that bird all in one go. We should have saved some of that.' He shook his head wistfully.

I peered under the car I was tied to and saw there wasn't enough room to squeeze beneath it. I was becoming wetter.

'Well, squirt,' Rumbo said with false jocularity, 'no sense in both of us getting wet. Think I'll get out of the rain.' He looked at me apologetically. I regarded him disdainfully, then turned my head away again.

' 'Er . . . I'll see you in the morning then,' he mumbled.

I watched him shuffle away. 'Rumbo,' I said.

He looked back at me, his eyebrows raised. 'Yes?'

'Do me a favour?'

'Yes?'

'Get neutered,' I said mildly.

'Good-night,' he replied, and trotted off to our nice warm bed.

The rain began to beat a rhythmic pattern on my body now and I curled up as small as I could, hunching my neck into my shoulders. It was going to be a long night.

Eleven

It was not only a long night but a disturbing one too. It wasn't just the discomfort of being drenched, for my fur held the moisture and formed a snug coating, keeping the worst of the chill away; but my sleep was nagged by memories.

Something had triggered the thoughts off and I didn't know what; it hid away somewhere in my mind's periphery. I saw a town — a village? I saw a house. Faces swam before me: I saw my wife, I saw my daughter. I was in a car; the human hands on the steering-wheel before me were my own. I drove through the town. I saw the angry face of a man I knew; he was also in a car and driving away from me. For some reason I followed. It was dark. Trees, hedges, flashed by, flat and eerie in the headlights. The car in front of me pulled in, turned into a narrow lane. I followed. It stopped; I stopped. The man I knew left his car and walked towards me. In the harsh glare from my headlights I saw his hand was outstretched — he was holding something? I opened my door as the hand pointed towards me. Then everything became a crystal of brilliant, glittering light. And the light became dark; and I knew nothing more.

Rumbo dropped a half-eaten roll in front of me. I sniffed at it and pulled out the thin slice of ham squashed between its crusty covers with my teeth. I gulped the meat down, then licked the butter from the bread. Then I ate the bread.

'You were yelping in your sleep last night,' Rumbo told me.

I tried to remember my dreams and after a while the fragments became whole pieces.

'Rumbo, I haven't always been a dog,' I said.

Rumbo thought before he spoke, then he said, 'Don't be silly.'

'No, listen to me, Rumbo. Please. We're not the same, you and I, not like other dogs. You're aware of that. Don't you know why?'

Rumbo shrugged. 'We're just smarter.'

'It's more than that. We still have the feelings, the thoughts of *men*. It's not just that we're more clever than other dogs – we remember how we *were*!'

'I remember being a dog always.'

'Do you, Rumbo? Don't you ever remember walking upright. Don't you remember having hands, having fingers that you could use? Don't you remember speaking?'

'We're doing that now.'

'No, we're not – not in men's language anyway. We're thinking now, Rumbo, we're making sounds, but our words are more thoughts than those sounds. Don't you see that?'

He shrugged again and I could see the subject bothered him. 'What difference does it make? I understand you, you understand me.'

'Think, Rumbo! Use your brain! Try to remember how it was before.'

'What's the point?'

This stopped me for a moment. Then I said, 'Don't you want to know why? How?'

'No,' he replied.

'But Rumbo, there has to be a reason. There must be some purpose to this.'

'Why?'

'I don't *know* why.' There was frustration in my voice now. 'But I want to find out!'

'Listen, squirt. We're dogs. We live like dogs, we're treated like dogs. We think like dogs. . . . ' I shook my head at this, but he continued: ' . . . and we eat like dogs. We're a little more intelligent than others, but we keep that to ourselves. . . . '

'Why don't we show them we're not like the rest?' I burst out.

'We *are* like the rest, squirt. We differ only in small ways.'

'That's not true!'

'It is true; you'll find out. We could show men how clever we are – lots of animals do. They usually end up in the circus.'

'It's not the same thing! That's only animals learning tricks.'

'Did you know they're teaching a chimpanzee to talk? Is that a trick?'

'How did *you* know that?'

Rumbo looked flustered.

'It was something you knew in the past, wasn't it, Rumbo? Not as a dog, but as a man. You read about it.'

'Read? What's read?'

'Words. Words on paper.'

'That's ridiculous, paper can't talk!'

'Nor can dogs.'

'We're talking.'

'Not in the same way as men.'

'Of course not. We're not men.'

'What are we?'

'Dogs.'

'Freaks.'

'Freaks?'

'Yes. I think we were men, then something happened and we became dogs.'

There was an odd look in Rumbo's eyes. 'I think the rain last night soaked into your brain,' he said slowly. Then he shook his body as if to shake off the conversation. 'I'm going to the park now. You could chew through the rope if you want to come.'

I slumped down on to the ground; it was obvious, as far as Rumbo was concerned, the discussion was over. 'No,' I said resignedly, 'I'll stay here till the Guvnor lets me loose. We don't want to make him any angrier.'

'Up to you,' said Rumbo and trotted off. 'I'll try and bring you something back!' he called out as he squeezed through the hole in the fence.

'Thanks,' I said to myself.

When the Guvnor turned up later that day he came over to see me. He shook his head a few times and called me a few more names. I tried to look pitiful and it must have had some effect, for he was soon untying the length of rope from my collar. He felt the dampness on my back and advised me to have a run to dry myself off. Accepting his advice, I shot out of the yard and made for the park where I knew I would find my companion. His trail was easy to follow but my progression from lamp-post to lamp-post was much more fun than just making straight for the park.

I found Rumbo sniffing round a little bitch, a skittish Yorkshire terrier, her lady owner anxiously trying to shoo my ragged friend away. Complex thoughts had gone: I couldn't understand Rumbo's interest in these silly lady dogs, but I did enjoy a good game. And this looked as though it could be a good game.

The weeks sped by – they may have been months – and I became lost in my canine world again, only occasionally being troubled by tormenting memories. Snow came, melted, was gone; winds swept in fiercely, spent their anger, and left meekly; the rain rained. The weather couldn't depress me, for I found its different moods interesting: I was experiencing things in a new way, with a different outlook; everything that happened was a *re*discovery. It was like the feeling you get after recovering from a long debilitating illness: everything is fresh and often startling; you observe with more appreciative eyes. You've known it all before, but familiarity has dulled things for you. That's the only way I can describe it.

Rumbo and I survived the worst winter could inflict comfortably enough. We had to travel further for our food, our surrounding area being a little too 'hot', but I enjoyed the excursions. We became firmer friends, since I was losing my overcharged puppy capriciousness and beginning to instigate some of our escapades rather than being led into them. Rumbo even called me Fluke now more often than squirt, for I was becoming almost as tall as him. When we weren't hunting for food or getting into mischief, Rumbo was off hunting bitches. He couldn't understand my lack of interest in the opposite sex and told me repeatedly I was old enough to feel some stirring in my loins at the scent of a ripe female body. I was puzzled myself, but really couldn't muster any inclinations whatsoever towards the female of my species; I suppose my instincts weren't yet canine enough.

Apart from that small concern and the occasional sudden flashes of my past life, the times were good; but like all good times, they had to end.

And end they did one dull and drizzly day.

Rumbo and I had just returned from the fruit market and were sniffing around a new vehicle which had been brought into the yard a few days before. It was a large dark-blue Transit van, and for some reason it had been parked at the rear of the yard. The lettering on its side had been sprayed out and I'd watched one of the workers change its number-plates the previous day. Its front bumper had been removed and replaced by a much sturdier one. Parked alongside was another car – a Triumph 2000 – and the number-plates on this had also been changed. Both vehicles were screened from the rest of the yard by the piles of wrecks. It was the smell from the van which attracted us – it must have been used to transport food at some time – but my human faculties should have made me aware of what was going on. The constant meetings in the hut between the Guvnor and his flashy cronies (meetings which had become even more frequent recently); the curious affluence of the Guvnor himself; his anger at having a policeman 'snooping' around some time before: it didn't take much of a brain to figure it all out. Unfortunately, mine wasn't even much of a brain.

We heard the yard gates being unlocked and then a car was driven into the yard. Rumbo raced through the maze of junk to find out who had arrived: to our surprise it was the Guvnor himself. It was a surprise to us because he was not an early bird, usually never arriving at the yard till mid-morning. He generally left it to his employees to open up and get on with the work by themselves.

The big man ignored us as we yapped around his legs while he unlocked the door to the hut. I noticed he'd discarded his sheep-skin for his old leather jacket and underneath he wore a dark-red polo-neck sweater. He was also wearing gloves, which was unusual for him. Throwing the butt of his cigar into the mud, the Guvnor entered the hut. No food for us today, then.

Rumbo and I mentally shrugged at each other and wandered off, but it wasn't long before the sound of more arrivals drew us back to the hut. A car pulled into the yard first and Lenny and another man got out, going straight into the hut, they too ignoring our wagging tails and eager expressions. Then three others arrived on foot.

A strange kind of tenseness had taken over the yard, making Rumbo and me nervous, edgy. The voices from inside the hut were muted, not the usual sounds of laughter or anger. This worried us even more.

After a short while the door opened and six men came out. The first four were now wearing dark grey smock-coats, the kind shopkeepers sometimes wear, and I saw they too were all wearing polo-necked sweaters. One man was just tugging the thick collar of his down from over his chin, suggesting that a moment before he'd been wearing it up to his ears. Lenny came out next, and although he wasn't wearing a smock he had on a polo-neck sweater. The Guvnor came out last and he still wore his leather jacket. They didn't speak as they passed, walking to the back of the yard, the nervous tension between them obvious and transferring to us, so that we became even more agitated. Lenny clucked his tongue at me and snapped his fingers in a half-hearted way, but ignored me when I bounded up to him.

We followed the six men round to the van. The back doors were opened and three of the smock-coated men climbed in, the fourth seating himself in the front. Before the Guvnor heaved his big frame into the passenger seat of the Triumph he said to the van driver: 'Right, you know what to do. Try and keep with us in the traffic, but if we get separated, you know where to meet up.' The driver nodded and the Guvnor turned away. Just before he slammed his door, he called out. 'Don't forget. You don't make your move till you see me wave my arm out the window.' The van driver thumbed up an acknowledgement.

Lenny was already in the driving seat of the Triumph and he suddenly gunned the engine. As the car crunched its way out of the yard, the big blue van following, I realised that for the first time I'd seen the Guvnor without a cigar sticking out of the corner of his mouth.

About an hour later the Triumph 2000 returned. It roared through the gates and drove straight round to the back of the yard. One of the yard's workmen ran to the gates and pushed them shut, then went back to his work as though nothing had happened.

Rumbo and I raced after the car and were just in time to see the Guvnor and Lenny clambering out. They ran round to the boot, opened it, and between them lifted out a large heavy-looking metal case. It had handles at each end and the two men used these to carry it round and into the hut. They returned to the car and pulled out four or five bulky sacks, and these too were hastily taken into the hut. The Guvnor locked the office door before they returned to the car. The men pushed us away angrily as we tried to clamber over them. There was an excited haste about them now – gone was the sullen nervousness of the morning – and this too was infecting us. A sharp whack on the nose kept me away, and Rumbo also took the hint.

'O.K., Lenny. Get shot of the motor,' the Guvnor said, taking a cigar from the inside pocket of his leather jacket. 'Don't worry about the smocks in the back – they don't matter now. You can dump it as far away as you like, but don't be drivin' around in it too long.'

'O.K., Guv,' Lenny said cheerfully. Before he turned on the ignition, the Guvnor poked another cigar through the open car window.

' 'Ere. You done well, boy. See you back 'ere Wednesday – not before!'

Lenny stuck the cigar into his mouth, grinned, put the car into gear, then moved off.

The front gate was just being opened for him by the same yard worker who'd closed it only minutes before when the police car screeched into the entrance, completely blocking Lenny's path. Doors flew open and suddenly there were blue uniforms everywhere. Another police car pulled up behind the first and more men in blue poured out.

Lenny was out of the Triumph in a flash, running for the back of the yard, his face white. The Guvnor, who was half-way back to his office when the police arrived, stood transfixed for a few seconds, then turned and bolted towards us. I can only guess that both he and Lenny intended to scale the corrugated-iron fence and make their getaway into the backstreets.

The latter didn't get as far as the former who, in the end, didn't get far at all. Lenny was brought down by a flying rugger tackle and was immediately engulfed in blue bodies. He screamed and cursed them but they wouldn't let him go.

Others gave chase to the Guvnor who had pounded past us now, throwing away his cigar as he went. The police shouted at him to stop, but he wasn't having any of it. He headed into the maze of wrecked cars.

Rumbo was both alarmed and angry. He didn't like these blue men: he didn't like them chasing his Guvnor. He growled at them and ordered them to stop. It did no good though – they weren't afraid of Rumbo. He jumped up at one and got a good grip on the policeman's sleeve, tugging and tearing at it with jerks of his body. The man went down and rolled over in the mud, taking Rumbo with him.

'No, Rumbo, no!' I cried out. 'Leave him alone! They'll hurt you!'

But Rumbo was too angry to listen. This was his territory, and the man they were after was the one he'd chosen to be his master. Another policeman kicked out at him, making him yelp in sudden pain and lose his grip on the uniform's sleeve. A stout wooden stick cracked across his nose and Rumbo staggered away from the sprawling policeman who immediately scrambled to his feet and joined in the chase after the Guvnor again.

'Are you all right?' I asked as I rushed over to Rumbo.

He moaned and his tail dropped between his legs. 'Get after them! Don't let them catch him!' He stumbled around shaking his head in a dazed way.

I dived into the alleyways separating the piles of damaged cars and pursued the pursuers. I could see the Guvnor ahead, climbing on to the bonnet of a car. He was grabbed from behind, but he kicked out with a vicious boot, knocking the unfortunate policeman on to his back. He scrambled up higher on to the roof of the car, then on to the bonnet of the car on top. If he crossed this pile of junk, it would take him close to the surrounding fence and he would be able to jump into the street below. The wreck he was climbing on to was unsteady, and it tottered precariously for a few sickening moments, nearly causing him to slither back down into the yard. He held tight and the car steadied itself. He began to climb again.

Two policemen began the ascent after the Guvnor while others headed in different directions in the hope of cutting him off. I couldn't just stand by and let them take the Guvnor; Rumbo had a loyalty to him and that meant I had too. I caught the seat of one of the climbing plod's trousers nicely with my teeth. I bit and pulled and he came tumbling down. He kicked out at me and beat me with his fists, but I was in a fury and hardly felt the blows.

Rumbo came in snarling and snapping, and the struggling policeman was forced to call on his companion for help. The dogs were tearing him to pieces, he screamed.

Well, we were being a bit rough, but we weren't savages (to tell the truth, it was a bit of a lark at that stage).

The second policeman jumped from the car bonnet into the mêlée and tried to separate man and dogs, flailing at us with his fists. This only made Rumbo more cross and he diverted his attention to the new assailant. More policemen were arriving by the second and I could see we'd stand no chance against such odds.

'It's no good, Rumbo!' I called out. 'There's too many!'

'Keep fighting, squirt,' he replied between mouthfuls of flesh and cloth. 'It's giving the Guvnor a chance to get away.'

It was no good. I felt a hand grasp my collar and I was yanked off my feet and thrown across the alleyway. I landed heavily against the boot of a car and fell to the ground badly winded. I gasped for breath and saw Rumbo receiving similar treatment. It took two policemen to deal with him, though.

By this time the Guvnor was on the roof of the second car and I could see him looking wildly around. He was being converged upon on all sides by blue uniforms and he yelled down defiantly as the police below began to climb up after him again.

'Look out!' one of them shouted. 'He's pushing the cars over!'

The policeman scrambled for safety and I saw that the Guvnor had stepped over on to the roof of the next semi-crushed car and was using a foot as a lever against the one he'd just left. It was already dangerously balanced and it didn't take much to send it toppling. The only thing was, the car the Guvnor was perched on toppled after it.

And worse, Rumbo had dashed forward again to ward off the pursuing policeman.

He couldn't have known what hit him; that was the only merciful thing about it. One minute he was crouched low, baring his teeth at the police, the next he had disappeared beneath a tumble of crushing metal.

'Rumbo!' I screamed, and dashed forward even before the crashing cars had had time to settle. 'Rumbo! Rumbo!'

I dodged around the twisted metal, trying to see beneath it, trying to find an opening to crawl through, willing my friend to be miraculously alive, refusing to accept the inevitable.

The thin stream of dark-red blood that came from beneath the cars jolted me into the truth of the situation: there was no chance at all for Rumbo.

I howled, the kind of howl you sometimes hear on an empty night from miles away; the cry of an animal at its lowest point of misery. Then I wept.

The Guvnor was in agony, his arm trapped deep between the two wrecks. He was lucky, though: it could have been his whole body.

A hand took me by the collar and dragged me gently away from the metal tomb, and I felt sympathy flowing from the policeman as he led me towards the front of the yard. I was too upset to resist. Rumbo was dead, and for the moment so was my will. I heard one of the officers tell someone to get an ambulance quickly; there was an injured man back there. I saw two men in plainclothes bringing the metal case from the hut and nodding towards another man questioning Lenny. Lenny was angry now, talking beligerently as he was held from behind by two uniformed men.

'Who done it then?' he was asking. 'Who fingered us?'

'We've had our eyes on this place a long time, son,' the man before him replied. 'Ever since one of our boys spotted Ronnie

Smiley's car in here awhile back. We all know what Ronnie gets up to, don't we, so we thought we'd wait awhile and let things run their course. Very interesting when we saw the stolen van coming in, then the car. Even more so when they didn't come out again – until this morning, that is.' He laughed at Lenny's obvious displeasure. 'Oh don't worry, it wasn't only that. We've had suspicions about this yard for a long time now. Wondered where your governor got his money from. Now we know, don't we?'

Lenny just looked away sullenly. The plainclothes policeman spotted me being led away.

'Funny thing is,' he remarked, 'the constable was only investigating a couple of thieving dogs when he spotted Smiley's car. Take after their master, don't they?' He nodded at the man holding firmly on to Lenny and they pushed him towards one of the police cars at the entrance to the yard. Before Lenny departed he gave me one last penetrating look that made me shiver inside.

And it was then that I knew where I was going. It pushed its way through befuddled layers and struck me almost physically.

I twisted my neck and snapped at the hand that held me. The startled policeman quickly drew his hand away – and I was loose. I bolted for the street and once again I was running, running, running.

But this time I had somewhere to go.

PART TWO

Twelve

How do you feel now? Is your mind still closed to my story, or are you wondering? Let me go on; there's a few hours before dawn.

My journey to Edenbridge was a long one, but strangely I knew the way as if I'd travelled that route many times before. When the town had been mentioned in the yard it had evidently planted a seed in my mind, and it was a seed that suddenly grew and sprouted. I wasn't sure what the town meant to me, whether it was where my home was or if it had some other significance, but I knew it was the place to go, the place to start from. What other alternative had I anyway?

I must have run for at least an hour, narrowly avoiding being run down by uncaring traffic more than once, before I reached a piece of waste ground where I was able to grieve for my lost friend in private. Creeping under a dumped sofa, its stuffing more out than in, I sank to the ground, resting my head between my paws. I could still see that trickle of blood running from beneath the rusted metal, forming a pool in a small dip in the earth and creating a miniature whirlpool, a vortex of Rumbo's life. Animals can feel grief just as deeply as any human, perhaps more so; they have limited ways of expressing their sorrow, though and their natural optimism usually enables recovery more quickly, there's the difference. Unfortunately, I suffered both as a human *and* an animal, and it was heavy stuff.

I stayed there until long into the afternoon, afraid and bewildered once again. Only my loyal companion, hunger, roused me into movement. I forget from where I scrounged food, just as I have forgotten a great deal of that long journey, but I know I did eat and was soon moving onwards. I travelled by night through the city, preferring the empty quietness of the streets, the activity of the day making way for the quiet prowlings of night creatures. I met many prowlers – cats, other dogs, spirits (so many in the streets of the city) and strange men who flitted in and out of the shadows as though light or open spaces would harm their bodies – but I avoided communication with any of them. I had a purpose and would allow nothing to distract me from it.

Through Camberwell, through Lewisham, through Bromley I went, resting during the day, hiding in derelict houses, parks or on waste ground – anywhere away from inquisitive eyes. I ate badly, for I took few risks; I didn't want to be sent back to a home, you see, not now I had an objective. I had become timid again now that Rumbo wasn't there to spur me on, to chastise me when I cowered, to threaten me when I balked and to laugh when I surprised him.

Soon I reached open country.

It rolled out before me, green and fresh under the gentle beginnings of spring. It wasn't true countryside yet, for I was only just outside the London suburbs, but after the blacks and the greys and the browns and the reds and the garishness of everything in the city, it seemed like passing through a barrier to where nature governed, and human influence played only a minor part. I was no longer afraid to travel by daylight.

The sudden strength of growing things thrilled me. Fresh green shoots thrust their way through the earth to breathe in fresh air, bulbs and tubers were sprouting and buds were breaking open on broad-leaved trees. Everywhere things were stirring, new life was being created. A vibrancy filled the air, filled my lungs and filled my limbs with its tingling life. The greens and yellows were newer, more dazzling, and the reds and oranges glowed with fire, sending out waves of energy. Everything glistened, everything shone with wetness. Everything was firm, vigorous, even the most delicate flower. It put new life into me.

I scrambled through a hedge running alongside the road, ignoring the scratchy protest of the thorny hawthorn and prickly dogrose. Two startled wrens screeched and froze as I brushed by their small huddled forms. A group of bright yellow stars flashed before me as I wormed my way through lesser celandine, plants which are the first in the queue for spring regeneration. I burst through into a field and ran like mad through its dewy wetness, twisting and rolling on to my back until my whole coat was soaked. I sucked at the grass, drinking the pure water from them, and dug holes in the soft earth to see what I could find. Beetles scuttled away from my inquisitive nose and a mole turned a blind eye. An eight-inch-long keeled slug curled its slick grey body into a ball as I sniffed at him and I quickly spat him from my mouth after a tentative taste. Cooked snails might be a delicacy for many, but raw slug isn't even fit for a dog.

My appetite soon returned, however, and I began to explore the field in search of food. I was lucky enough to find a young rabbit nibbling at the bark of a tree and unlucky enough to be unable to catch him. I cursed his speed then wondered if I could have killed the rabbit even had I caught up with him. I'd never killed for food before.

Fortunately, I found some late winter fungus among a group of trees and devoured the upturned yellow caps and stalks with relish, somehow aware that the mushrooms were not poisonous. Was this animal instinct or had I some human knowledge of fungi? The question bothered me for only a second or so, for a sleepy wood-mouse shuffled lazily between my legs, his black little eyes searching the ground for snails. I felt no urge to eat or fight him, but I did give his reddish-brown back a playful tap with my paw. He stopped, looked up at me, then ambled on at the same pace, ignoring me totally. I watched him go then decided it was time to move on myself, the diversion pleasant enough but hardly profitable as far as self-discovery was concerned. I raced back across the field, scrambled through the hedge, and set off down the road again.

It wasn't long before I found myself back among shops and houses, but I kept on, pausing only once to steal an apple from a splendid display outside a fruiterer's. The road became more and more familiar to me now that the complications of the city streets were far behind, and I knew it was a route I must have taken many times before.

By the time I'd reached Keston my pads were very sore, but I kept going until I reached a small place called Leaves Green. There I rested through the cold night in a small wood, nervous of the country night noises, my unease finally driving me to seek shelter in somebody's front garden. I felt more comfortable being in range of human contact.

I didn't eat much the following day, but I won't bore you with the various misadventures that befell me in my search for sustenance; suffice to say, by the time I reached Westerham, I'd have bitten the leg off a cow.

It was at Westerham that a nasty experience was awaiting me. And this I must tell you about.

Thirteen

Church bells woke me. They had a strident Sunday morning sound that sent my thoughts racing back to other times – human times.

Awareness of my present plight dismissed the memories before they gathered pace and I stretched my aching limbs, wincing at the tenderness of my foot-pads as I pushed them against the ground. A bus shelter had been my refuge for the night, but the early morning chill had crept into my bones and seemed reluctant to leave. I yawned and my stomach grumbled for nourishment. Glancing around, I saw there were no shops in the immediate vicinity, so I trotted gingerly along the street keeping my nose high in the air, acutely receptive for the faintest waft of food smells. I soon found myself in the High Street and to my dismay realised it was indeed Sunday, for all the shops – apart from a couple of newsagents – were closed. It was a pretty dismal dog who stood shivering by the kerbside, looking first left then right, undecided, unwanted and unfed.

It was the pealing bells that gave me the idea. Small groups of people were walking briskly towards the sound, clad in Sunday best, a brightness about them that would wear off as the day wore on. Children held hands with parents or skipped along ahead of them; grannies clutched at the elbows of middle-aged offspring; sombre husbands walked stiffly alongside beaming wives. There was a fresh friendly feeling in the air, the beginning of spring enhancing the Sunday morning ritual, encouraging goodwill to all men. And maybe dogs, too.

I followed the people to their church. It was on a hill, half hidden away from the road by a screen of trees, its entrance reached by a gravelly path winding through a surrounding graveyard. A few of the people clucked their tongues at me or gave me a friendly pat as they passed by, but soon they had all disappeared into the cold, grey-stoned building. I settled down on a flat gravestone to wait.

I enjoyed the muted singing that came from the church immensely, occasionally joining in at the bits I knew. The service seemed to go on forever, and I soon became bored with the long stretches of silence between hymns so I began to explore the churchyard and was surprised at the thriving animal and insect life in this place of the dead. The unmistakable sound of the congregation rising as one body inside the church drew me away from my fascinating study of a rainbow-coloured spider's web, and I trotted back round to the enormous doorway, keeping to the damp grass which was so cool to my sore pads. I waited to one side of the porch and soon the flock came pouring out, some looking uplifted, others looking relieved now that their weekly duty was done. It was one of the uplifted members I wanted.

I soon spotted her: a little old lady, probably in her mid-sixties, round-faced, smiling constantly, knowing and known by everybody, it seemed. All lace and kindness. Perfect.

She spent several minutes chatting to the vicar, occasionally breaking off from her conversation to call hello to a passing acquaintance, giving them a little blessing with her white-gloved hand. I waited patiently until she'd ended her dialogue with the cleric then followed her as she made her way through the remaining gossiping cliques. Smiling sweetly and stopping to chat to every third or fourth person she finally drew clear of the throng and strode spritely down the gravel path. I followed, keeping a few yards behind, not ready to make my move while she still had so many distractions. We reached the road and she turned left, climbing further up the steep hill and away from the town.

'Good morning, Miss Birdle!' the people we passed called out, and she acknowledged them with a cheery wave.

Now's the time, I thought, and scampered up ahead of her. I stopped four yards ahead, turned to face her and gave her my sweetest smile.

'Woof,' I said.

Miss Birdle threw her hands up in surprise and beamed with delight. 'What a pretty dog!' she exclaimed and I wagged my rump with pride. She advanced on me and clasped my head between white-gloved hands.

'Oh, what a lovely boy!' She rubbed my back and I tried to lick her face, congratulating myself on finding another Bella. 'Yes, yes, he is!' she went on.

After a few moments of unbridled affection she bade me good-bye and strode on, waving at me as she went. I bounded after her and tried to leap into her arms, slobbering and grinning and desperately trying to fawn my way into her heart and charity. I admit it: I had no shame.

Miss Birdle gently pushed me down then patted my head. 'Off you go, now, there's a good dog,' she said in her kind way.

Sorry Rumbo, but at that point I whimpered.

Not only that, I hung my head, drooped my tail and looked cow-eyed at her. I was pathetic.

It worked, for she suddenly said, 'Oh my poor dear, you're starving, that's what it is! Look at those skinny old ribs.' My chin almost touched the ground as I hammed up my perform-ance. 'Come along then, dear, you come with me and we'll soon put you to rights. Poor little wretch!'

I was in. I tried to lick her face again in glee, but she restrained me with a surprisingly firm hand. I needed no encouragement to follow her, although she seemed to think I did, for she con-stantly patted her thigh and called out 'Come along now.'

She had plenty of energy, this charming old lady, and we soon reached a rusty iron gate, behind which was a muddy path lead-ing away from the road. Tangled undergrowth lay on either side of the narrow path and there was a constant rustling of hidden life as we made our way along it. I sniffed the scent of Miss Birdle along this well-used route, not the fresh powdery smell that fol-lowed in her wake now, but a staler version of it mingled with the scents of many animals. Now and again I stopped to explore a particularly interesting odour, but her call would send me scam-pering onwards.

112

Suddenly we emerged into a clearing and a flint-walled cottage stood before us, its corners, door and window openings reinforced by cut stone. It was a beautiful scene – like walking on to a chocolate box – and in perfect character with Miss Birdle herself. Smug with my own cleverness, I trotted up to the weathered door and waited for Miss Birdle to catch up with *me*.

She pushed open the door without using a key and beckoned me to enter. In I went and was pleased to find the interior of the cottage matched the quaintness of the exterior. Ancient furniture, worn and comfortable, filled the main room in which I found myself, there being no hallway. Well-cared for ornaments were scattered around the room, one of those interesting dark-wood dressers filled with delicately painted crockery taking up a large part of one wall. I wagged my tail in approval.

'Now let's just see if you've an address on your collar, then we'll give you some food, eh?' Miss Birdle placed her handbag on a chair and leaned forward over me, reaching for the name-plate on my collar. I obligingly sat down, determined not to kill any golden geese through over-exuberance. She peered short-sightedly at the scratched lettering on the nameplate and tutted in mild annoyance at herself.

'My old eyes are getting worse,' she told me, and I smiled in sympathy. I would dearly have loved to have told her of my own peculiarly clear eyesight, of the many changing colours I could see in her face, of the blue deepness in her ageing eyes, of the sparkling colours all around us, even in her faded furniture. It was frustrating to have to keep these things to myself, and even Rumbo had been unable to understand my visual sensitivity.

She felt inside her handbag and produced a light-rimmed pair of spectacles and muttered 'That's better,' as she put them on. She still squinted through the lenses but managed to make out the name on the strip of metal.

'Fluke,' she said. 'Fluke. That's a funny name for a dog. And no address. Some people are very careless, aren't they? I haven't seen you around before, I wonder where you've come from? Bet you've run away, haven't you? Let me look at your footies . . . ' She lifted a paw. 'Yes, they're sore, aren't they? You've come a long way. Been badly treated, haven't you? Thin as a rake. It isn't right.'

My hunger was making me a little impatient by now and I whimpered again, just to give her the idea.

'Yes, yes. I know what you want, don't I? Something for your tummy?' It's a pity people have to talk to animals as though they were children, but I was in a forgiving mood and willing to put up with a lot more than baby-talk. I thumped my tail on the carpet in the hope that she would take that for an affirmative to her question. 'Course you do,' she said. 'Let's get you something.'

The kitchen was tiny, and lying in a basket on the floor, fast alseep, was Victoria.

Victoria was the meanest, surliest cat I've ever come across, either before or since that time. Now these feline creatures are renowned for their tetchiness, for they believe they're a race apart from other animals and well above you lot, but this monster took the prize. She sat bolt upright, her fur bristling and her tail ramrod-straight. She hissed disgustedly at me.

'Take it easy, cat,' I said anxiously. 'I'm only passing through.'

'Now you settle down, Victoria,' said Miss Birdle, equally anxious. 'This poor doggie is starving. I'm just giving him something to eat, then we'll send him on his way.'

But it's no good trying to talk sense to a cat, they just won't listen. Victoria was out of her basket in a flash, up on to the sink and through the half-open kitchen window.

'Oh dear,' sighed Miss Birdle, 'you've upset Victoria now,' and then this nice old lady gave me a hefty kick in the ribs.

I was so shocked I thought I'd imagined it, but the pain in my side told me otherwise.

'Now let's see what we've got,' Miss Birdle said thoughtfully, her index finger in the corner of her mouth as she looked up into the cupboard she'd just opened. It was as though nothing had happened and I wondered again if anything actually had. The throb in my side assured me something had.

I kept a safe distance between us after that and watched her warily when she placed a bowl of chopped liver before me. The food was delicious but marred by my sudden nervousness of the

114

old lady I just couldn't understand what had happened. I licked the bowl clean and said thank you, very aware of my manners now. She fondled my ears and chuckled approvingly at the empty bowl.

'You *were* hungry, weren't you?' she said. 'I'll bet you're thirsty now. Let's give you some water.' She filled the same bowl with water and placed it before me again. I lapped it up greedily.

'Now you come with me and rest those poor weary legs.' I followed her back into the main room and she patted a hairy rug in front of the unlit fire. 'Rest there, nice and comfy, and I'll just light the fire for us. It's still too cold for my old bones, you know. I like the warm.' She prattled on as she put a match to the already laid fire, her words soft and comforting. I became confident again, sure that the strange incident which had taken place in the kitchen was merely a slight lapse on her part, caused by the shock of seeing her beloved pet cat leaping through the window. Or maybe she'd slipped. I dozed off as she sat in the armchair before the fire, her words lulling me into a warm feeling of security.

I woke in time for lunch, which wasn't much, she being an old lady living on her own, but she gave me a good portion of it. The cat returned and was further put out at the sight of me gobbling down food which she felt was rightfully hers. However, Miss Birdle made a big fuss of her, running into the kitchen and returning with an opened tin of catfood. She poured some of it on to a small plate and laid it before the sour-faced mog. With a menacing look at me, Victoria began to eat in that jerky cat fashion, neatly but predatorily, so unlike the clumsy, lip-smacking manner of us dogs. My portion of Miss Birdle's lunch was soon gone and I casually sauntered over to Victoria to see how she was doing, ready to help her clean her plate, should the need arise. A spiteful hiss warned me off and I decided to sit at Miss Birdle's feet, my face upturned and carefully composed into an expression of mild begging. A few tasty morsels came my way, so my fawning was not in vain. This disgusted the cat even more, of course, but her sneers didn't bother me at all.

After Miss Birdle had cleared the table and washed up, we settled in front of the fire once again. Victoria kept an aloof distance and came over to settle on the old lady's lap only after much enticement. We all dozed, I with my head resting on my benefactor's slippered feet. I felt warm and content – and more secure than ever before. Perhaps I should stay with this kind old lady and forget my quest, which might just bring me more misery. I could be happy here; the cat would be a mild annoyance but nothing to worry about. I needed some human kindness, I needed to belong to someone. I'd lost a good friend and the world was a big and lonely place for a small mongrel dog. I could always search out my other past at some future time when I learned to live as I was. I could offer Miss Birdle companionship. I could guard her home for her. I could have a permanent meal-ticket.

These thoughts ran through my head as I dozed, and I made the decision that I would stay there for as long as possible – little suspecting what lay in store for me.

Later on, Miss Birdle stirred and began to get ready to go out. 'Never miss the afternoon service, my dear,' she told me.

I nodded approvingly, but didn't stir from my cosy position. I heard the old lady bustling around upstairs for a while, then the clomp of heaving walking shoes as she descended the stairs. She appeared in the doorway, resplendent in white gloves and a dark-blue straw hat. Her suit was pink and her high-necked blouse a bright emerald green. She looked dazzling.

'Come along, Fluke, time for you to go now,' she said.

My head shot up. What? Go?

'What? Go?' I said.

'Yes, time for you to go, Fluke. I can't keep you here, you belong to someone else. They may have looked after you badly, but you do belong to them. I could get into trouble by keeping you here, so I'm afraid you've got to leave.' She shook her head apologetically then, to my dismay, grabbed my collar and dragged my resisting body to the door. For an old lady she was quite strong, and my paws skidded along the wood floor as I tried to hold back. Victoria enjoyed every moment, for I could hear her snickering from her perch on the window-sill.

'Please let me stay,' I pleaded. 'Nobody owns me. I'm all alone.'

It was no use: I found myself outside on the doorstep. Miss

Birdle closed the door behind us and marched down the path, calling me to follow. Having no choice, I followed.

At the gate she patted my head and gave me a little push away from her. 'Off you go now,' she urged. 'Home. Good boy, Fluke.'

I wouldn't budge. After a while she gave up and marched down the hill away from me, looking round twice to make sure I wasn't following her. I waited patiently until she was out of sight then pushed my way back through the gate and padded down the muddy path to the cottage. Victoria scowled through the window as she saw me coming and shouted at me to go away.

'Not likely,' I told her as I squatted on my haunches and prepared to wait for the old lady's return. 'I like it here. Why should you have it all to yourself?'

'Because I was here first,' Victoria said crossly. 'You've got no right.'

'Look, there's plenty for both of us,' said I, trying to be reasonable. 'We could be friends.' I shivered at the thought of being friends with this miserable specimen but was prepared to ingratiate myself for the sake of a nice secure home. 'I wouldn't get in your way,' I said in my best toadying voice. 'You could have first and biggest share of all the food' (until I was better acquainted with the old lady, I thought). 'You can have the best place to sleep' (until I have wormed my way into Miss Birdle's affections), 'and you can be the head of the house, I don't mind' (until I get you alone some day and show you who the real boss is). 'Now, what do you say?'

'Get lost,' said the cat.

I gave up. She would just have to lump it.

An hour later Miss Birdle returned and when she saw me sitting there she shook her head. I gave her my most appealing smile.

'You *are* a bad boy,' she scolded, but there was no anger in her voice.

She let me go into the cottage with her and I made a big fuss of licking her heavily stockinged legs. The taste was horrible, but when I decide to smarm, there are no limits. I was sorry not to have the dignity of Rumbo, but there's nothing like insecurity to make you humble.

117

Well, I stayed that night. And the following night. But the third night – that's when my troubles started all over again.

At nine-thirty in the evening Miss Birdle would turn me out and I would dutifully carry out my toilet; I knew that was expected of me and had no intention of fouling things up (excuse the play on words – couldn't help it). She would let me back in after a short while and coax me into a small room at the back of the cottage which she used to store all sorts of junk. Most of it was unchewable – old picture frames, a pianoforte, an ancient unconnected gas cooker, that sort of thing. There was just enough room for me to curl up beneath the piano keyboard and here I would spend the night, quite comfortable although a little frightened at first (I cried that first night but was O.K. the second). Miss Birdle would close the door on me to keep me away from Victoria who slept in the kitchen. The cat and I were still not friends and the old lady was well aware of it.

On that third night she neglected to close the door properly; the catch didn't catch and the door was left open half an inch. It probably wouldn't have bothered me, but the sound of someone creeping around during the night aroused my curiosity. I'm a light sleeper and the soft pad of feet was enough to disturb me. I crept over to the door and eased it open with my nose; the noise was coming from the kitchen. I guessed it was Victoria mooching around and would have returned to my sleeping-place had not those two agitators, hunger and thirst, begun taunting my greedy belly. A trip to the kitchen might prove profitable.

I crept stealthily from the room and made my way through the tiny hallway into the kitchen. Miss Birdle always left a small lamp burning in the hallway (because she was nervous living on her own, I suppose) and had no trouble finding the kitchen door. It, too, was open.

Pushing my nose round it, I peered into the gloom. Two slanting green eyes startled me.

'That you, Victoria?' I asked.

'Who else would it be?' came the hissed reply.

I pushed in further. 'What are you doing?'

'None of your business. Get back to your room.'

But I saw what she was doing. She had a small wood-mouse trapped between her paws. Her claws were withdrawn so she was obviously playing a fine teasing game with the unfortunate creature. His reddish-brown back was arched in paralytic fear and his tiny black eyes shone with a trance-like glaze. He must have found his way into the cottage in search of food. The absence of house-mice (undoubtedly owing to Victoria's vigilance) would have encouraged him and he must have been too stupid (or too hungry) to have been aware of the cat's presence. Anyway, he was well and truly aware of it now, and paying nature's harsh price for carelessness.

He was too scared to speak so I spoke up for him.

'What are you going to do with him?'

'None of your business,' came the curt reply.

I made my way further into the kitchen and repeated my question. This time a wheezy snarl was the reply.

It's not in an animal's nature to have much sympathy for his fellow creatures, but the plight of this defenceless little thing appealed to the other side of *my* nature; the human side.

'Let him go, Victoria,' I said quietly.

'Sure, after I've bitten his head off,' she said.

And that's what she tried to do, there and then, just to spite me.

I moved fast and had Victoria's head between my jaws before she had a chance to dodge. We spun around in the kitchen, the mouse's head in the cat's mouth, and the cat's head in mine.

Victoria was forced to drop the terrified wood-mouse before she had done any real damage and I saw with satisfaction the little creature scurry away into a dark corner and no doubt down a dark hole. Victoria squealed and pulled her head from my jaws, raking my brisket as she did so. I yelped at the stinging pain and lunged for her again – very, very angry now.

Round and round that kitchen we ran, knocking chairs over, crashing against cupboards, shouting and screaming at each other, too far gone with animal rage to concern ourselves with the noise we were making and the damage we were doing. At one point I snapped my teeth round Victoria's flailing tail and the cat skidded to a forced halt, a scream of surprise escaping her.

She wheeled and drew her sharp claws across my nose and I had to let go, but her tail was now bald near the tip. I sprang forward again and she leapt upwards on to the draining-board, knocking down the pile of crockery left there to dry by Miss Birdle. It came crashing down, shattering into hundreds of pieces on the stone floor. I tried to leap on to the draining-board myself and almost succeeded, but the sight of Victoria diving head-first through a pane in the closed window amazed me so much I lost my concentration and slipped back on to the floor. I'd never seen a cat – or any animal – do *that* before!

I was still half lying there, perplexed, and a little delighted, I think, when the white-gowned figure appeared in the kitchen doorway. I froze for a second at the apparition, then realised it was only Miss Birdle. Then I froze again.

Her eyes seemed to glow in the darkness. Her white hair hung wildly down to her shoulders and the billowy nightdress she wore crackled with static. Her whole body quivered with a rising fury that threatened to dismantle her frail old body. Her mouth flapped open but coherent words refused to form; she could only make a strange gargling sound. However, she did manage to reach up a trembling hand to the light switch and flick it on. The increased light suddenly made me feel very naked lying there among the smashed crockery.

I gulped once and began to apologise, ready to blame the cat for everything, but the screech that finally escaped the old lady told me words would be wasted at that particular moment. I scooted beneath the kitchen table.

It didn't afford me much protection unfortunately, for one of those dainty slippered feet found my ribs with fierce accuracy. It found my ribs a few more times before I had the sense to remove myself. Out I shot, making for the open doorway, scared silly of this dear old thing. This dear old thing then threw a chair at me and I yelped as it bounced off my back. She came at me, arms and legs flailing, stunning me into submission, terrifying me with her strength. My collar was grabbed and I found myself being dragged back to the cluttered 'guest' room. I was thrown in and the door slammed shut behind me. From the other side of the heavy wood I heard language I'd been used to in the Guvnor's yard but hardly expected to hear in a quaint old cottage and from such a sweet old lady. I lay there trembling, fighting desperately to keep a grip on my bowels and bladder: I was in enough disgrace without *that*.

Another miserable night for me. I must be unique in knowing the full meaning of the expression 'a dog's life'. I know of no other animal who goes through so many highs and lows of emotion as the dog. Maybe we make trouble for ourselves; maybe we're over-sensitive; or maybe we're just stupid. Maybe we're too human.

I hardly slept. I kept expecting the door to swing open and the ancient demon to appear and deal out more punishment. But it didn't swing open; in fact, it didn't swing open for another three days.

I whined, I howled, I grew angry and barked; but nothing happened. I messed on the floor and cried because I knew it would get me into trouble. I starved and cursed the mouse who'd got me into this predicament. My throat grew sore because I had nothing to drink and I cursed the malicious cat who'd caused this situation. My limbs grew stiff because of lack of exercise and I cursed Miss Birdle for her senility. How could she change from being a charming, delicate old lady one moment into a raging monster the next? All right, I know I was to blame to some extent – her cat *had* gone head-first through the window – but was that enough reason to lock me up and starve me? Self-pity sent me into a sulk that occasionally welled up into anger, then receded into a sulk again.

On the third day the door handle rattled, twisted and the door slowly opened.

I cowered beneath the pianoforte hardly daring to look up, prepared to take a beating with as little dignity as possible.

'There, there, Fluke. What's the matter then?' She stood smiling down at me, that sweet granny smile, that gentle innocence which only belongs to the very old or the very young. I snuffled and refused to be lured out.

'Come on then, Fluke. All's forgiven.'

Oh yes, I thought, until your next brainstorm.

121

'Come and see what I've got for you.' She left the doorway and disappeared into the kitchen, calling my name in her enticing way. A meaty smell came my way and, tail drooped between my legs, I made my way cautiously after her. I found Miss Birdle pouring a whole tin of dogfood into a bowl on the floor.

I might be unforgiving but my stomach has a mind of its own and it insisted I go forward and eat. Which I did of course without too much inner conflict, though I kept a wary eye on the old lady all the time. The food soon went and so did the water that followed, but my nervousness took a little longer to disappear. Victoria watched me all the time from her basket in the corner, flicking her tail in a slow, regular movement of cold fury. I ignored her but was actually pleased to see she'd come to no real harm by diving through the window. (I was also pleased to see the bald tip of her tail.)

I shied away when Miss Birdle reached down to me, but her calm words soothed my taut nerves and I allowed her to stroke me and soon we were friends again. And we remained friends for at least two weeks after that.

Victoria made a point of keeping out of my way and, I confess, I made a point of keeping out of hers, too. I would scamper down to the town with Miss Birdle when she went shopping and always did my best to behave myself on these occasions. The temptation to steal was almost irresistible, but resist it I did. I was reasonably well fed and the dreadful incident of my fight with Victoria was soon forgotten. Miss Birdle introduced me to all her friends (she seemed to know everybody) and I was made a great fuss of. In the afternoons I would romp in the fields behind the cottage, teasing the animals living there, inhaling the sweetness from the budding flowers, revelling in the growing warmth from the sun. Colours zoomed before me, new smells titillated my sense: life became good once more and I grew healthier. Two weeks of happiness, then that rat of a cat managed to upset everything again.

It was a sunny afternoon and Miss Birdle was in her garden at the front of the cottage tending her awakening flowerbeds. The front door was open and I trotted backwards and forwards through it, enjoying the luxury of having a home where I could come and go as I pleased. On my third or fourth trip, Victoria wandered in after me, and I should have realised something was going to happen when she slyly started a conversation with me. Being a fool and eager to make friends, I readily laid my suspicions to one side and answered her questions, settling down on the rug, prepared to have a good natter. As I said before, cats, like rats, aren't much given to conversation and I was pleased Victoria was making the effort on my behalf, thinking she had accepted me as a permanent guest and was trying to make the best of things. She asked me where I came from, if I knew any other cats, if I liked fish – all sorts of inconsequential questions. But all the time her yellow eyes were darting around the room as though looking for something. When they rested upon the huge dresser with all its fine crockery she smiled to herself. Then came the insults: What was a mangey-looking thing like me doing here, anyway? Were all dogs as stupid as me? What made me smell so? Little things like that. I blinked hard, startled by this sudden change in attitude. Had I offended her in some way?

She came closer so we were almost nose to nose, and stared intently into my eyes. 'You're a dirty, snivelling, fleabitten, worm-riddled mutt. You're a thief and a scoundrel!' Victoria looked at me with some satisfaction. 'Your mother was a jackal who coupled with a hyena. You're vulgar and you're nasty!'

Now there are many insults you can throw at a dog and get away with, but there's one we will not put up with, one word that really offends us. That's right – *dirty*! (We often are, of course, but we don't like to be told so.) I growled at her to be quiet.

She took no notice, of course, but ranted on, throwing insults not worth repeating here, but some quite ingenious for one of her limited vocabulary. Even so, I would probably have borne all these insults had she not finally spat in my face. I went for her, which is exactly what she had wanted all along.

Up into the dresser she went, spitting and howling. I tried to follow her, shouting at the top of my lungs, finding some nice insults of my own to call her. Victoria backed away along the dresser as I tried in vain to reach her and, as she moved her body backwards, so the ornamental plates which stood balanced upright on the first shelf came tumbling down.

A shadow fell across the doorway but the half-wit (that's right) carried on barking at the wailing cat. I only became fully aware of Miss Birdle's presence when the rake came down heavily on my back. I scooted for the front door, but the old lady had sprung wings on her heels and reached it before me. She slammed it shut and turned to face me, the rake clutched in her gnarled old hands like a lance, its iron-toothed end almost touching my nose. I looked up at her face and gulped loudly.

It had gone a deep purple, the tiny broken veins seeming to explode like starbursts across her skin, and her once kind eyes pressed against their sockets as though about to pop out and roll down her cheeks. I moved a fraction of a second before she did and the rake crashed into the floor only inches behind me. We did a quick circuit of the room while the cat looked on from her safe perch on the dresser, a huge smug smile on her face. On our third lap round, Miss Birdle spotted her and took a swipe at her indolent body with the rake (I suppose the frustration of not being able to catch me had something to do with it). It caught the cat a cracking blow and she shot off the dresser like a ball from a cannon and joined me in the arena. Unfortunately (more so for us), Miss Birdle's sweeping blow at Victoria had also dislodged more plates, together with a few hanging cups and a small antique vase. They followed the cat but of course refused to join us in our run; they lay broken and dead where they had fallen.

The anguished scream from behind told us matters had not improved: Miss Birdle was about to run amuck! Victoria chose the narrow cave formed between the back of the settee and the wall below the front window to hide in. I pushed my way in behind her, almost climbing on to her back in my haste. It was a tight squeeze but we managed to get half-way down the semi-dark corridor. We trembled there, afraid to go further because that would lead us out again.

'It's your fault!' the cat snivelled.

Before I had a chance to protest, the long handle of the rake found my rump and I was suddenly pushed forward in a most painful and undignified way. We became a confused tussle of hairy bodies as we now struggled to reach the other end of the narrow tunnel, violent pokes from the rear helping us achieve our

124

goal. We emerged as one and the old lady dashed round to meet us.

Being the bigger target, I came in for the most abuse from the rake, but it pleases me to tell you the cat received a fair share. The chase went on for another five minutes before Victoria decided her only way out was up the chimney. So up she went and down came the soot – clouds and clouds of it. This didn't improve Miss Birdle's humour one bit, for the soot formed a fine black layer on the area around the fireplace. Now it was the old lady's habit to lay that fire every morning and light it when she settled down in the afternoon, even though the warmer weather had arrived, but for once she decided to bring her schedule forward. She lit the fire.

I gazed on in horror as the paper flamed and the wood chips caught. Forgetting about me for the moment, Miss Birdle settled down in her armchair to wait, the rake lying across her lap in readiness. We stared at the fireplace, Miss Birdle with grim patience, I with utter dismay. The room around us was now a shambles, all cosiness gone.

The flames licked higher and the smoke rose. A spluttered cough fell down with more soot and we knew the cat was still perched there in the dark, unable to climb any further. Miss Birdle's rigid lips turned up at the corners into a rigid smile as we waited, the silence broken only by the crackling of burning wood.

A knock at the door made us both jump.

Miss Birdle's head swung round and I could see the panic in her eyes. The knock came again and a muffled voice called out, 'Miss Birdle, are you in?'

The old lady burst into action. The rake was shoved behind the settee, overturned chairs were righted, and broken crockery was swept beneath the armchair. Only the soot-blackened carpet and a slight disarray of the room gave evidence that something out of the ordinary had happened. Miss Birdle paused for a few seconds, tidied up her clothing, rearranged her personality, and went to the door.

The vicar's hand was raised to knock again and he smiled apologetically down at Miss Birdle.

'So sorry to disturb you,' he said. 'It's about the flower arrangements for Saturday's fête. We can count on your wonderful assistance again this year, can we not, Miss Birdle?'

The old lady smiled sweetly up at him. 'Why, of course, Mr Shelton. Have I ever let you down?'

The change in her was remarkable; the demon castigator had reverted back to the aged angel of innocence. She simpered and fawned over the vicar and he simpered and fawned with her; and all the while the cat roasted in the chimney.

'Now how is that little stray fellow of yours?' I heard the vicar inquire.

'Oh, he's thoroughly enjoying his stay,' Miss Birdle replied, having the nerve to turn round to me and smile. 'Come here, Fluke, and say hello to the vicar.'

I suppose I was expected to run over and lick the clergyman's hand, wagging my tail to show how pleased I was to see him, but I was still in a state of shock and could only cower behind the armchair.

'Oh, he doesn't like strangers, does he?' the vicar chuckled.

I wasn't sure if he was talking to me or Miss Birdle, for his voice had taken on that simpleton's tone people usually reserve for animals. They both gazed at me affectionately.

'No, Fluke's very shy of people,' said Miss Birdle, melting butter clogging her words.

'Have the police located his owner yet?' the vicar asked.

'Constable Hollingbery told me only yesterday that nobody had reported him missing, so I suppose whoever owned Fluke didn't really want him very much.'

They both tutted in harmony and looked at me with soul-churning sympathy.

'Never mind,' the vicar said brightly. 'He has a good home now, one I'm sure he appreciates. And I'm sure he's being a very good doggie, isn't he?' The question was aimed directly at me.

Oh yes, I thought, and the pussy is being a very good pussy, albeit a well-cooked one.

'Oh dear, Miss Birdle, the room seems to be filling with smoke. Is your chimney blocked?'

126

Without turning a hair, the old lady gave a little laugh and said, 'No, no, it always does that when it's first lit. It takes a while before the air begins to flow properly.'

'I should have it seen to, if I were you, mustn't spoil such a charming abode with nasty smoke, must we? I'll send my handyman around tomorrow to fix it for you. Now the Woman's Guild committee meeting next Wednesday . . . ' And that was when Victoria dropped from her hiding-place.

The vicar stared open-mouthed as the soot-covered, fur-smoking cat fell down into the fire, screaming and spitting with rage, leapt from the fireplace and streaked for the door. She flew past him and he could only continue to stare as the smouldering black body disappeared down the path leaving a jet-stream of trailing smoke behind. His mouth still open, the vicar turned his attention back to his elderly parishioner and raised his eyebrows.

'I *wondered* where Victoria had got to,' said Miss Birdle.

The cat never came back, at least not while I was still there, and I seriously doubt she ever returned. Life in the cottage went on in its crazy normal way, the incident forgotten by my benefactor as though it had never happened. Several times in the ensuing week Miss Birdle stood at her front door and called out Victoria's name, but I guess the cat was several counties away by then (I still have bad dreams of her being out there in the night, watching me, smouldering in the dark). However, Miss Birdle soon forgot about Victoria and directed all her attention towards me, but, not surprisingly, I felt I could never really trust her. I spent my time nervously waiting for the next eruption, treading very warily and learning to subdue my undisciplined spirits. It occurred to me to leave, but I must confess the lure of good food and a comfortable bed was stronger than my fear of what might happen next. In a word, I was stupid (Rumbo had been right), and even I'm amazed at just how stupid my next mistake was.

I found a nice, chewy plastic object lying on the edge of the kitchen-sink drainer one night. The kitchen was my night-time domain now that Victoria was gone and her basket had become my bed. I often had a poke around during the night or in the early hours of the morning and this time I had been lucky in finding something to play with. Not too hard, not too soft, and crunchy when I bit down firmly. No good to eat, but pretty to look at with its pink surface and little white frills around one edge. It kept me amused for hours.

When Miss Birdle came into the kitchen next morning, she showed no sign of being amused at all. Her toothless mouth opened to let the raging soundless cry escape, and when I looked into that gummy mouth, the human part of me realised what lay chewed, twisted and splintered between my paws.

'My teefth!' Miss Birdle spluttered after her first wordless outcry. 'My falthe teefth!' And that old gleam came back into her eyes.

Stupid I am, yes, and stupid enough to amaze even myself, right. But there comes a time in even the most stupid dog's life when he knows exactly what he should do next. And I did it.

I went through that window just as the cat had (through the new window-pane, in fact), terror helping me achieve what I had been unable to do before (namely, getting on to that kitchen sink). The fact that Miss Birdle was reaching for the long carving knife which hung with its culinary companions on the wall convinced me this might be her worst brainstorm yet. I thought it unnecessary to wait and find out.

I went over her flowerbeds, scrambled through bushes and undergrowth and burst into the open fields beyond, a terrifying image of Miss Birdle in her long white nightdress chasing after me and brandishing the wicked carving knife keeping me going for quite some distance. It's certainly handy to have four legs when you're constantly running away.

I was a long way from that cottage before I collapsed into an exhausted heap, and had already resolved never to return. It was no way for even a dog to live. I shuddered at the thought of the schizophrenic old lady, so charming one minute, so lethal the next. Were all her friends fooled by her antique sweetness, her enchanting old maidishness? Didn't anybody see what lurked just behind that veneer, ready to be unleashed by the slightest provocation? I presumed not, for she seemed so popular and respected by her townsfolk. *Everybody* loved Miss Birdle. And

Miss Birdle loved *everybody*. Who would ever guess that the endearing old lady had the slightest streak of viciousness in her? Why should anyone think such a thing? Knowing her lovable side so well, even I had difficulty in believing her kindness could turn to such violence, but I shall never trust any sweet old ladies again. How do you explain such a twist in human nature? What made her good one moment, bad the next? It's quite simple really.

She was nuts.

Fourteen

Dog's life, dogsbody, dogfight, dog-eared, dog-days, dog-end, dirty dog, mad dog, lazy dog, dog-tired, sick as a dog, dog-in-the-manger, underdog – why so many abuses of our name? You don't say hedgehog's life, or rabbit's body, or frog-in-the-manger. True, you do use certain animal names to describe a particular type of person – chicken (coward), monkey (rogue), goose (silly) – but they're only individual descriptions, you never extend the range with a particular species. Only dogs come in for this abuse. You even use various species' names in a complimentary manner: an elephant never forgets (not true), happy as a lark (not true), brave as a lion (definitely not true), wise as an owl (are you kidding?). But where are the dog compliments? And yet we're cherished by you and regarded as man's best friend. We guard you, we guide you; we can hunt with you, we can play with you. You can even race some of our breed. You use us for work and we can win you prizes. We're loyal, we trust, and we love you – even the meanest of you can be adored by your dog. So why this derogatory use of our name? Why can't you be 'as free as a dog', or 'as proud as a dog', or 'as cunning as a dog'? Why should an unhappy life be a dog's life? Why should a skivvy be called a dogsbody? Why wouldn't you send *even* a dog out on a cold night? What have *we* done to deserve such blasphemy? Is it because we always seem to fall into some misfortune or other? Is it because we appear foolish? Is it because we're prone to over-excitement? Is it because we're fierce in a fight but cowardly when our master's hand is raised against us? Is it because we have dirty habits? *Is it because we're more like you than any other living creature?*

Do you recognise our misfortunes as being similar to your own, our personalities a reflection of yours but simpler? Do you pity, love and hate dogs because you see your own humanness in us? Is that why you insult our name? Are you only insulting yourselves?

'A dog's life' had true meaning for me as I lay there in the grass, panting. Was my life always to follow this unlucky pattern? It was the human part of my nature coming to the fore again, you see, for not many animals philosophise in such a way (there are exceptions). Fear and that good old human characteristic, self-pity, had aroused the semi-dormant side of my personality once more and I thought in terms of man yet still with canine influence.

I shook off my misery the way dogs do and got to my feet. I had an objective which had been neglected; now was the time to continue my search. It was a beautifully fresh day and the air was filled with different scents. I was without a patron again and still without a friend but because of it I was free; free to do as I pleased and free to go where I pleased. I had only myself to answer to!

My legs broke into an unpremeditated sprint and once again I was in full flight, only this time my compulsion to run was ahead of me and not behind. I knew the direction I should take instinctively and soon found myself back on the road and heading towards the town that had sounded so familiar.

Cars swished past at frequent intervals, causing me to shy away. I was still very frightened of these mechanical monsters even after months of living in the busy city, but somehow I knew I had once driven such a vehicle myself. In another life. I came to a heavily wooded area and decided to take a small detour, knowing it would actually cut a few miles off my journey.

The wood was a fascinating place. It hummed with hidden beings which my eyes soon began to detect, and to which (surprisingly) I was able to put names. There were beetles, gnats, hoverflies, tabanad flies, mosquitoes, wasps and bees. Speckled wood and brimstone butterflies fluttered from leaf to leaf. Dormice, wood-mice and bank-voles scuttled through the undergrowth, and grey squirrels were everywhere. A woodpecker stared curiously at me from his perch and ignored my hearty good morning. A startled roe-deer leapt away as I stumbled into its hiding-place. Thousands on thousands of aphides (you might know them as blackfly or greenfly) sucked the sap from leaves and plant stems, excreting honeydew for ants and others to feed on. Birds – songthrush, chaffinch, great tit, blue tit, jays and many, many more – flew from branch to branch or dived into the undergrowth in search of food. Earthworms appeared and disappeared at my feet. I was amazed at the teeming activity and a little in awe of it, for I had never realised so much went on in these sheltered areas. The colours almost made my eyes sore with their intensity and the constant babble of animal chatter filled my head with its raucous sound. It was exhilarating and made me feel very alive.

I spent the day exploring and thoroughly enjoyed myself, seeing things through new eyes and with a completely different mental approach, for I was now part of that world and not merely a human observer. I made a few friends here and there, although I was generally ignored by this busy population of animals, insects, birds and reptiles. Their attitudes were quite unpredictable, for I had quite a pleasant chat with a venomous adder, whereas a cute-looking red squirrel I chanced upon was extremely rude. Their appearance bore no resemblance to their nature. (My conversation with the adder was strange, for snakes, of course, have only an inner ear which picks up vibrations through the skull. It made me realise again that we were communicating through thought.) I discovered snakes are a much-maligned creature for this one was a very inoffensive sort, as have been most I've come into contact with since.

For once I forgot about my belly, and allowed myself to enjoy my surroundings, sniffing out trails left or boundaries marked by various animals through their urine and anal glands. I marked my own trail from time to time, more as a 'Fluke was here' sign than a means of finding my way back. There'd be no going back for me.

I dozed in the sun in the afternoon and when I awoke I wandered down to a stream to drink. A frog sat there eating a long pink worm, scraping the earth off the shiny body with his fingers as he swallowed. He stopped for a moment and regarded me curiously, the poor worm frantically trying to work his body back out of the frog's mouth. The frog blinked twice and resumed his eating, the worm slowly disappearing like a live string of spaghetti. The worm's tail (head?) wriggled once more before leaving the land of the living, then was gone, the frog's eyes bulging even more as he gulped convulsively.

'Nice day,' I said amiably.

He blinked again and said, 'Nice enough.'

I wondered briefly how he would taste but decided he didn't look too appetising. I seemed to remember from somewhere that his legs might be quite tasty, though.

'Haven't seen you around here before,' he commented.

'Just passing through,' I replied.

'Passing through? What does that mean?'

'Well . . . I'm on a journey.'

'A journey to where?'

'To a town.'

'What's a town?'

'A town. Where people live.'

'People?'

'Big things, on two legs.'

He shrugged. 'Never seen them.'

'Don't people ever pass this way?'

'Never seen them,' he repeated. 'Never seen a town, either. No towns here.'

'There's a town not too far off.'

'Can't be any such thing. Never seen one.'

'No, not here in the woods, but further away.'

'There is no other place.'

'Of course there is. The world's far bigger than just this woodland!'

'What woodland?'

'Around us,' I said, indicating with my nose. 'Beyond these nearby trees.'

'There's nothing beyond those trees. I only know those.'

'Haven't you ever gone further than this glade?'

'What for?'

'To see what else there is.'

'I know all there is.'

'You don't. There's more.'

'You're mistaken.'

'You've never seen me before, have you?'

'No.'

'Well, I come from beyond the trees.'

He puzzled over this for a minute. 'Why?' he said finally. 'Why have you come from beyond the trees?'

'Because I'm passing through. I'm on a journey.'

'A journey to where?'

'To a town.'

'What's a town?'

'Where people . . . oh, forget it!'

He did, instantly. The frog wasn't really that concerned.

I stomped away, exasperated. 'You'll never turn into a handsome prince!' I shouted over my shoulder.

'What's a handsome?' he called back.

The conversation made me ponder over the animals' point of view. This amphibian obviously thought that the world was only that which he could see. It wasn't even that there was nothing beyond, for he had never even asked himself the question. And it was that way for all animals (apart from a few of us): the world consisted of only what they knew – there was nothing else.

I spent a restless and anxious night beneath an oak tree, the sound of an owl and its mate keeping me awake for most of the night. (It surprised me to discover the 'to-whit-to-whoo' was a combination of both birds – one hooted while the other twitted.) It wasn't so much their calling to each other that bothered me, but their sudden swoops down on to vulnerable voles scurrying around in the dark below, the sudden screech culminating in the victim's squeal of terror which disturbed and frightened me. I didn't have the nerve to upset the owls, since they seemed vicious and powerful creatures, nor did I have the courage to wander around in the dark looking for a new sleeping-place. However, I did eventually fall into an uneasy sleep and the following morn-

ing I went hunting for chickens with my new friend, (I thought)
– a red fox.

I awoke to the sound of yapping. It was still dark – I estimated
dawn was a couple of hours away yet, and the yaps came from
not too far off. Lying perfectly still, I tried to detect in which
direction the yaps came from, and from whom. Were there pups
in this wood? Sure that the owls were now at rest, I inched my
way forward away from the trees, my senses keened, and had
not gone far when I came across the fox's earth in a hollow under
a projecting tree-root. A musty smell of excrement and food
remains hit my nostrils and then I saw four sets of eyes gleaming
out at me.

'Who's there?' someone said in a half-frightened, half-
aggressive, manner.

'Don't be alarmed,' I reassured them hastily. 'It's only me.'

'Are you a dog?' I was asked, and one set of eyes detached itself
from the others. A fox skulked forward out of the gloom and I
sensed rather than saw she was a she. A vixen.

'Well?' she said.

'Er, yes. Yes, I'm a dog,' I told her.

'What do you want here?' Her manner had become menacing
now.

'I heard your pups. I was curious, that's all.'

She seemed to realise I was no threat and her attitude relaxed
a little. 'What are you doing in these woods?' she asked. 'Dogs
rarely come in here at night.'

'I'm on my way . . . somewhere.' Would she understand what
a town was?

'To the houses where the big animals live?'

'Yes, to a town.'

'Do you belong to the farm?'

'The farm?'

'The farm on the other side of the woods. Over the meadows.'
Her world was larger than the frog's.

'No, I don't belong there. I'm from a big town, a city.'

'Oh.'

The vixen seemed to have lost interest now and turned back when a small voice called from the darkness.

'Mum, I'm hungry!' came the complaint.

'Be quiet! I'm going soon.'

'I'm hungry too,' I said, and I really was.

The vixen's head swung back to me. 'Then go and find yourself some food!'

'Er . . . I don't know how to in a forest.'

She looked at me incredulously. 'You can't feed yourself? You can't find yourself a rabbit, or a mouse, or a squirrel?'

'I've never had to before. I mean, I've killed rats and mice, but nothing bigger than that.'

She shook her head in wonder. 'How have you survived, then. Coddled by the big ones, I suppose – I've seen your kind with them. They even use you to hunt us!'

'Not me! I'm from the city. I've never hunted foxes.'

'Why should I believe you? How do I know you're not trying to trick me?' She showed me her pointed teeth in a grin that wasn't a grin but a threat.

'I'll go away if you like, I don't want to upset you. But perhaps me and your mate can go and find some food for all of us.'

'I don't have a mate any more.' She spat the words out and I could feel the anger and hurt in them.

'What happened to him?' I asked.

'Caught and killed,' was all she would say.

'Find us some food, Mum,' came the plaintive cry again.

'Well, perhaps I could help *you*,' I suggested.

'Huh!' scoffed the vixen, then her voice changed. 'There may be a way you can be used, though,' she said thoughtfully.

I stiffened to attention. 'Anything. I'm starving.'

'All right, then. You kids stay here and don't go outside! You hear?'

They heard.

'Come on, you.' The fox brushed past me.

'Where too?' I asked eagerly, following behind.

'You'll see.'

'What's your name?' I called out.

'Hush up!' she whispered fiercely, then said, 'What's a name?'

'What you're called.'

'I'm called fox. Vixen to be exact. You're called dog, aren't you?'

'No, that's what I am. Fox is what you are. I'm called Fluke.'

'That's daft. Flukes are flatworms!'

'Yes, but men called me Fluke – it's an expression.'

She shrugged off my silliness and didn't speak again till we'd walked for at least a mile and a half. Then she turned to me and said, 'We're nearly there now. You have to keep very very quiet from here on – and move very carefully.'

'Right,' I whispered, trembling with excitement.

I could see the farm stretched out before us and from the stench I guessed it was mainly a dairy farm.

'What are we going to do – kill a cow?' I asked in all serious-ness, the excitement draining from me.

'Don't be daft!' the fox hissed. 'Chickens. They keep chickens here too.'

That's all right then, I thought. That could be quite interest-ing.

We crept towards the farm and I copied the fox's style exactly, running forward silently, stopping, listening, sniffing, then padding forward again, from bush to bush, tree to tree, then stealthily through the long grass. I noticed the wind was coming towards us, bringing lovely rich farmyard smells. We reached a huge open shed and slid easily into it. On our left were the remaining bales of last winter's barley straw, and on our right bags of fertiliser piled high. When we emerged, I stopped at a water-trough and, resting my paws on its edge, had a good tongue-lapping drink.

'Come on!' the vixen whispered impatiently. 'No time for that. It'll be dawn soon.'

I padded after her, feeling quite refreshed now, every nerve alive and dancing. The fox and I passed through the collection yard, over the feeding-troughs, by the silage pit, then past a nearly empty but pungent manure hold. I wrinkled my nose – you can have too much of a good thing – and sped after the wily fox. We could hear the cows snoring in their enormous shed, and the smell of barley managed to cover the smell of manure (although not entirely) as we went by a giant barley bin. We were soon through the yard and I could see the dark outline of a house in the moonlight ahead of us.

The fox stopped and sniffed the air. Then she listened. After a while, her body relaxed slightly and she turned to me.

'There's one of your sort here, a big ugly brute. We must be careful not to wake him – he sleeps up near the house. Now this is what we'll do. . . . ' She came closer to me and I saw she was quite attractive really in a sharp-looking way. 'The chickens are over in that direction. A thin but sharp barrier keeps them in and us out. If I can get a good grip with my teeth at the bottom of the barrier, I can pull it up so we can get underneath. I've done it before – it's just a knack. Once we get in, all hell will break loose . . . ' (did she understand the concept of hell or was it only my mind translating her thoughts) ' . . . and when it does, we'll only have a short time to grab a hen each and make a bolt for it.'

I'm sure her eyes must have gleamed craftily in the dark, but I was too excited – or too dumb – to notice.

'Now,' the vixen went on, 'when we run for it, we must go separate ways. That will confuse the big dog and the big thing who keeps him. The two-legged thing . . . '

'Man,' I said.

'What?'

'Man. That's what he's called.'

'Like Fluke?'

'No. That's what he is. Man.'

The vixen shrugged. 'All right. Man has got a long stick that screams. It kills too – I've seen it kill – so you must be careful. You had better run back this way through the yard because there's plenty of cover, and I'll go the other way across the fields at the back because I'm probably faster. O.K.?'

'Right,' I said keenly. Rumbo was probably turning over in his grave just then.

On we stalked, silently and breathlessly, and before long we'd reached the chicken-coop and its surrounding wire-mesh fence. It wasn't a particularly large coop – the farmer probably only kept chickens as a sideline, his profit coming from his cows – but it could have contained thirty to fifty hens. We heard an occasional flutter from inside, but it was obvious they hadn't detected our presence.

The vixen scuffled around at the base of the wire fencing and tried to get a grip on it with her teeth. She managed to do so and pulled upwards with all her strength. The wiring tore loose from its wooden base, but my companion was unable to keep her grip and it fell back down again, although it remained loose. There had been a ripping sound as the wire mesh tore loose and the noise had alerted the hens inside the hutch. We could hear them moving around inside. Soon they would be jabbering and screeching.

The fox tried again and this time she was more successful. The wiring sprang up and sank back only slightly when she released it.

'Quickly,' she whispered and shot through the opening. I tried to follow, but my body was bigger than the fox's and the wire cut into my back, trapping me half-way through. Meanwhile, the fox had climbed up a short run, lifted a small flap with her nose, and in a flash was inside the hutch. The screams and the thrashing sounds that came from inside paralysed me. The sudden deep barking that came from somewhere near the house made me mobile again. I struggled to get free, knowing the farmer and his 'screaming stick' would soon be down there.

The small hatch to the chicken-hutch suddenly flew open and out poured the squawking poultry, feathers and bodies flying through the air like torn pillow-cases.

Now I don't know if you know this, but hens, as do many groups of animals, have their own hierarchy. It's called the 'pecking order', and the hen who has the biggest and meanest peck is the boss, the second meanest pecker is under the first, but boss over the others, and so on all the way down the line. But now it looked as though everyone was equal.

They all ran around like lunatics and the only competition was who could fly the highest.

The fox emerged, a hen as big as her own body fluttering feebly in her grasp. She ran towards the gap where I was crouched neither in nor out.

139

'Move yourself,' came her muffled command.

'I'm stuck!' I yelled back.

'The dog's coming, quickly!' she said, desperately pacing backwards and forwards along the side of the pen. But the dog must have been chained, for although we could hear him barking, he was still nowhere near. Then we heard the roar of the farmer as a window flew open back there at the house.

That moved me. With a terrific wrench backwards I tore myself free of the wire, scratching my back nastily as I did so. The fox, chicken and all, was through in a flash.

'You go that way!' she shouted at me, feathers spraying from her mouth.

'Right!' I agreed. And then I ran up towards the house, towards the dog, towards the farmer and his gun, while my friend flew off in the opposite direction.

I was half-way there before I stopped and said to myself, Hold on! I looked round just in time to see a fleeting black shape tearing across a field before being swallowed up by the dark line of a hedge.

I turned back as I heard the door of the house crash open and out leapt the farmer wearing vest and trousers and heavy boots. The sight of the long object he held in two hands before him nearly made me faint. The other dog was going mad now trying to get at me and I saw it was a very healthy looking mastiff. I had the feeling his stretched chain would break at any moment.

I groaned and wondered which way to run. The end of the cowshed lay to my left, outhouses to my right. Ahead was the farmer and his monster dog. There was only one way to go really, and of course the fox had taken it. I turned in my tracks and made for the open fields.

A choking kind of shout came from the farmer as he saw me and I heard him lumber out into the yard. I didn't have to look to know he was raising the gun to his shoulder. The blast told me it was a shotgun and the whistling over my ears told me the farmer wasn't a bad shot. My speed increased as my quickening heartbeat acted as a crazy metronome to my legs.

More footsteps, silence, and I waited for the second blast. I swerved as much as I could and crouched low to make myself as small a target as possible. The hens leapt into the air in horror as I passed them, no doubt thinking I had returned for second helpings.

I leapt into the air myself as my tail seemed to explode into shreds. I yelp-yelped in that rapid way dogs do when they're hurt, but kept going, relieved that I could actually keep going. The barking behind me reached a new frenzy and then I knew the mastiff had been let loose, for the sound took on a new, more excited pitch. The welcoming fields rushed forward to meet me and I scrambled under a fence and was into them, my tail on fire.

'Gorn boy!' came the shout from behind and knew the monster dog was closing up on me. The field seemed to stretch out before me in the moonlight and grow wider and longer, the hedge on the far side shrinking rather than growing. The mastiff hadn't caught up with me yet, but his heavy panting had. He'd stopped barking to save his breath and conserve his energy. He really wanted me, that dog.

I inwardly cursed myself for being so stupid and allowing myself to be used as a decoy by the fox. It made me very angry and almost caused me to turn and vent my anger on the pursuing dog. Almost, but not quite – I wasn't *that* stupid.

The mastiff seemed to be panting in my left ear now and I realised he was very close. I turned my head quickly to see just how far behind he was and immediately wished I hadn't – his grinning teeth were level with my left flank!

I swerved just as he took a snap at me and he went sailing on by, rolling over on the grass as he endeavoured to stop himself. The mastiff came racing back and I went racing on again, so he found himself running in the wrong direction once more.

Looming up ahead was the hedge and I was grateful it had stopped playing shrinking tricks on me. I dived into it and prayed I wouldn't hit a tree trunk; the mastiff plunged in right behind me. Brambles tore at us and startled birds complained of the noise, but we were through in an instant and tearing across the next field. Knowing he would soon catch up, I began my swerving tactics again. Fortunately, the mastiff wasn't too bright and he fell for my tricks every time. It was exhausting though and several times his teeth raked across my flank, but eventually even his energy seemed to be depleting. On one very successful twist he had gone at least five yards beyond me, so I stopped for a breather. The mastiff stopped too and we both faced each other across the grass, our shoulders and chests heaving with the effort.

'Look,' I panted, 'let's talk about this.'

But he had no inclination to talk at all. He was up and at me, growling as he came. So on I went.

As I ran, I picked up a scent. Foxes are usually pretty smart when it comes to covering their tracks – they'll double back, climb trees, jump into water, or mingle with sheep – but when they've got a dead chicken in their mouth, dripping blood and feathers, it's another story. She'd left a trail as strong as cat's-eyes in a road.

The mastiff got a whiff of it and momentarily lost interest in me, then we both tore off down that smelly path. Through another hedge we went, and then we were in the wood, dodging round trees and heavy clumps of bushes. Startled night creatures scurried back to their homes as we crashed past, twittering and protesting at our intrusion.

I don't think the mastiff's night vision was as good as mine – probably he was a lot older – because his progress wasn't so fast, and several times I heard him cry out when he bumped into trees. I gained some distance on him and began to feel a little more confident about getting away. Then I bumped into the fox.

The hen had hampered her flight and she must have dropped it at this point and paused to retrieve it. I bore no malice – I was too frightened at what lay behind – and would probably have ignored her had I not gone straight into her crouching body. We rolled over in a struggling heap, fox, chicken and dog, but parted immediately when the mastiff joined us. He bit out at everything within reach and, fortunately for both the vixen and me, we were able to leave him there with a mouthful of chicken, content in his catch as he shook the dead body and tried to rip it apart. The farmer would be well pleased when his guard dog returned with a mouthful of feathers and blood.

We went our separate ways, the vixen and I, she back to her cubs, me to find somewhere quiet to nurse my wounds. It was growing lighter by the minute now and I hurried to get away from the area, not sure of my directions but wanting to travel as far as possible before daybreak. I knew (how did I know?) farmers took great pains to seek out and destroy any killer dogs who plagued their livestock and this particular farmer would certainly regard me as such. My tail stung terribly now, over-riding the hurt from my various other wounds, but I didn't dare stop and examine the damage. I came to a stream and swam across, enjoying the coolness on my wounds, and when I reached the other side, clambered out with reluctance. I gave myself a good shake then sped onwards, determined to get clear of the farmer's land.

The sun had risen and was gathering strength by the time I stumbled into a resting-place. I ached and I hurt, and all I could do was lay there in a dip in the ground and try to recover my strength. After a while I was able to twist my head and examine my throbbing tail. The wound wasn't half as bad as I expected; only the very tip had been damaged and much of the hair had gone from it. Victoria would have been pleased, for our tails were now a good match. The sting from the scratches on my back and flanks caused by the wire mesh and the mastiff's teeth weren't too bothersome, but irritating nonetheless. I rested my head between my paws and slept.

When I awoke, the sun was high overhead and covering my body with its warmth. My mouth and throat felt dry and my wounds were a dull throb. My stomach grumbled over the lack of food. Rousing myself, I looked around and saw I was resting in the dip of a gentle slope. A valley spread out below and other grassy hills rose up on the other side, their soft summits mounted by beech copses. I wandered down hoping to find a spring at the bottom of the hill, nibbling at certain grasses as I went. The grass – sheep's fescue it's called – wasn't too tasty, but I knew many downland animals ate it, so at least it would provide nourishment. Again, I wondered how I knew about such things: how I knew the snail I'd just pushed was a Roman snail that used calcium in the chalky downland soil to make its shell; how the bird that sang somewhere to my right was a skylark; how the butterfly that fluttered by was an Adonis blue wakened prematurely by the sudden warm weather. I had obviously taken a keen interest in the countryside in my past life and taken the trouble to learn about nature and her ways. Had I perhaps been a naturalist or a botanist? Or had it been only a hobby to me? Maybe I had been brought up in the countryside and names and habits came naturally to me. I shook my head in frustration: I had to find out *who* I had been, *what* I had been; how I had died and why I had become a dog. And I had to discover who the man was, the man in my dreams who seemed so evil, who seemed such a threat to my family. My family — the woman and the little girl — I had to find them, had to let them know I wasn't dead. Had to tell them I'd become a dog. Wasn't there someone who could help me?

There was. But I wasn't to meet him till two nights later.

Fifteen

Pay attention now because this is important. This is the point in my story where I heard a reason for my existence, why I was a dog. This is the part that may help you if you're prepared to accept it. I won't mind if you don't, it's up to you, but bear in mind what I asked of you at the beginning: keep your mind open.

I wandered on for two more days, finding the road again and relieved to find it. I was determined not to waste any more time, but to find my home and to find some answers.

Road signs were becoming more difficult to read; I had to gaze at them for a long time and concentrate hard. However, I found the right way and continued my journey, pleased to reach a town further on; it was much easier for me to get food when I was among people and shops. A few people took pity on me in my bedraggled state (although others chased me away as though I were something unclean) and gave me scraps. I spent the night with a family who took me in, and I think they had intentions of keeping me as a pet, but the following morning when they let me out to relieve myself, I ran off to the next town. I hated spurning this family's kindness, but nothing could deter me from my purpose now.

I was less successful in scrounging food in the next town, although I still ate adequately enough. The road was becoming more and more familiar and I knew I was nearing my home. My excitement grew.

When dusk fell I was between towns, so I left the roadside and entered a deep wood. Hungry (of course) and tired (naturally), I searched for a safe place to sleep. I don't know if you've ever spent the night in a wood alone, but it's very creepy. It's pitch-black for a start (no street lights), and there's a constant rustling and cracking of dry twigs as the night animals mooch around. My night vision's good – better than yours – but even so, it was still difficult to detect much in the darkness. Eerie glowing lights set my heart racing until I investigated and discovered a couple of glow-worms going through their meeting routine. Another blue-green glow upset me until I realised it was only honey fungus growing on a decaying tree-trunk.

I could hear bats flapping around, their high-pitched squeals making me jump, and a hedgehog trundled into me and pricked my nose with its spikes. I considered going back to the roadside, but the blinding lights and roaring engines of passing cars were even more frightening.

The woods at night are almost as busy as in the daytime, except everything seems even more secretive. I adopted this secretive attitude myself and skulked around as stealthily as I could in search of a resting-place. Finally I discovered a nice soft mound of earth beneath a thick roof of foliage, just under a tree. It made a snug hiding place and I settled down for the night, a strange feeling of portentousness filling me. My instincts were right, for later that night my sleep was disturbed by the badger.

And it was the badger who explained things to me.

I had failed to fall into a comfortable sleep and lay dozing in the dark with my eyes constantly blinking open at the slightest sound. A shifting of earth behind me made me jump and twist my head round to see the cause of the disturbance. Three broad white lines appeared from a hole in the sloping ground and a twitching nose at the base of the middle stripe sniffed the air in all directions.

It stopped when it caught my scent.

'Who's there?' a voice said.

I didn't reply – I was ready to run.

The white lines widened as they emerged from the black hole. 'Funny smell,' the voice said. 'Let me see you.'

I now saw there were two shiny black eyes on either side of the middle stripe. I realised it was a badger speaking, and it was, two *black* stripes running down his white head which gave him this white-striped appearance. I backed away, aware that these creatures could be fierce if alarmed or angered.

'Is it . . . is it a . . . dog? Yes, it's a dog, isn't it?' the badger guessed.

I cleared my throat, undecided whether to stay or run.

'Don't be afraid,' the badger said. 'I won't cause you any bother unless *you* mean us harm.' He waddled his great coarse-haired body out of his sett and I saw he was at least three feet long and very tall.

'Yes, I thought I recognised the smell. We don't get many dogs in here on their own. You are on your own, aren't you? You're not night-hunting with one of those cattle farmers, are you?'

Like the fox, he didn't seem to trust the dog's association with man. I found my voice and nervously assured him I wasn't.

He seemed puzzled for a moment and I felt rather than saw him regard me curiously. Whatever was going on in his mind was interrupted as another badger shuffled from the sett. I assumed this was his sow.

'What's going on? Who's this?' came a sharp voice.

'Hush now. It's only a dog and he means us no harm,' the boar told her. 'Why are you alone in the woods, friend? Are you lost?'

I was too nervous to speak up right then and the sow piped up again: 'Chase him away! He's after the babies!'

'No, no,' I managed to say. 'No, please, I'm just passing through. I'll be on my way now. Don't get upset.' I turned to trot off into the darkness.

'Just a moment,' the boar said quickly. 'Stay awhile. I want to talk to you.'

Now I was afraid to run.

'Chase him away, chase him away! I don't like him!' the sow urged.

'Be quiet!' the boar said quietly but firmly. 'You go on about your hunting. Leave a good trail for me to follow – I'll join you later.'

The sow knew better than to argue and huffed her way rudely past me, emitting a vile odour from her anal glands as a comment.

'Come closer,' the boar said when his mate had gone. 'Come where I can see you better.' His enormous body had shrunk and I realised his hair must have become erectile on seeing me and had now returned to its normal smoothness. 'Tell me why you're here. Do you belong to a man?'

I shuffled forward, ready to flee.

'No, I don't belong to anyone. I used to, but don't any more.'

'Have you been mistreated?'

'It's a lucky dog who hasn't.'

He nodded at this. 'It would be a fortunate animal *or* man who hasn't,' he said.

It was my turn to regard him curiously. What did *he* know of man?

The badger settled himself into a comfortable position on the ground and invited me to do the same and, after a moment's hesitation, I did.

'Tell me about yourself. Do you have a man name?' he asked.

'Fluke,' I told him, puzzled by his knowledge. He seemed very human for a badger. 'What's yours?'

The badger chuckled drily. 'Wild animals don't have names, we know who we are. It's only men who give animals names.'

'How do you know about that? About men, I mean.'

He laughed aloud then. 'I used to be one,' he said.

I sat there stunned. Had I heard right? My jaw dropped open.

The badger laughed again, and the sound of a badger laughing is enough to unnerve anyone. Fighting the urge to run I managed to stammer, 'Y-you used . . . '

'Yes. And you were too. And so were all animals.'

'But . . . but I know *I* was. I thought I was the only one! I . . . '

He stayed my words with a grin. 'Hush now. I knew you weren't like the others at my first whiff of you. I've met some who have been similar, but there's something very different about you. Calm down and let me hear your story, then *I'll* tell you a few things about yourself – about us.'

I tried to still my pounding heart and began to tell the badger about my life: my first recollections in the market, my first owner, the dogs' home, the breaker's yard, the Guvnor, Rumbo, the old lady, and my episode with sly old fox. I told him where I was going, of my man memories and, as I went on, my nerves settled, although an excitement remained. It was wonderful to talk in this way, to tell someone who would listen, who understood the things I said, how I felt. The badger remained quiet throughout, nodding his head from time to time, shaking it in sympathy at others. When I had finished, I felt drained, drained yet strangely elated. It seemed as though a weight had been lifted. I was no longer alone – there was another who knew what I knew! I looked eagerly at the badger.

'Why do you want to go to this town – this Edenbridge?' he asked before I could question him.

'To see my family, of course! My wife, my daughter – to let them know I'm not dead!'

He was silent for a moment, then he said, 'But you are dead.'

The shock almost stopped my racing heart. 'I'm not. How can you say that? I'm alive – not as a man, but as a dog. I'm in a dog's body!'

'No. The man you were is dead. The man your wife and daughter knew is dead. You'd only be a dog to them.'

'Why?' I howled. 'How did I become like this? Why am I a dog?'

'A dog? You could have become any one of a multitude of creatures – it depended largely on your former life.'

I shook my body in frustration and moaned, 'I don't understand.'

'Do you believe in reincarnation, Fluke?' the badger asked.

'Reincarnation? Living again as someone else, in another time? I don't know. I don't think I do.'

'You're living proof to yourself.'

'No, there must be another explanation.'

'Such as?'

'I've no idea. But why should we come back as someone or something – *else*?'

'What would be the point of just one existence on this earth?'

'What would be the point of two?' I countered.

'Or three, or four? Man has to learn, Fluke, and he could never

149

learn in one lifetime. Many man religions advocate this, and many accept reincarnation in the form of animals. Man has to learn from all levels.'

'Learn what?'

'Acceptance.'

'Why? Why should he learn acceptance? What for?'

'So he can go on to the next stage.'

'And what's that?'

'I don't know, I haven't reached it. It's good, I believe. I feel that.'

'So how do you know this much? What makes *you* special?'

'I've been around for a long time, Fluke. I've observed, I've learned, I've lived many lives. And I think I'm here to help those like you.'

His words were soft and strangely comforting, but I fought against them. 'Look,' I said, 'I'm confused. Are you saying I have to accept being a dog?'

'You have to accept whatever life gives you – and I mean *accept*. You have to learn humility, Fluke, and that comes only with acceptance. Then will you be ready for the next level.'

'Wait a minute,' I said, taking on a new tact out of desperation. 'We *all* become animals when we die?'

He nodded. 'Nearly all. Birds, fishes, mammals, insects – there are no rules as to which species we're born into.'

'But there must be billions upon billions of living creatures in the world today. They can't all be reincarnated humans, our civilisation just hasn't been going that long.'

The badger chuckled. 'Yes, you're right. There are at least a million known animal species, over three quarters of which are insects – the more advanced of us.'

'Insects are the more advanced?' I asked in a flat tone.

'That's right. But let me answer your first point. This planet of ours is very old and it's been washed clean many times so that life can start all over again, a constant cycle of evolvement which allows us to learn a little more each time. Our civilisation, as you call it, has not been the first by any means.'

'And these . . . these people are still coming back, still . . . learning?'

'Oh yes. Much of our progress owes itself to race memory, not inspiration.'

'But no matter how long ago it all began, man evolved from animals, didn't he? How could animals have been reincarnated humans if they were here first?'

He just laughed at that.

You can imagine the state I was in by now: half of me wanted to believe him because I needed answers (and he spoke in such a soothing, matter-of-fact way), and the other half wondered if he was demented.

'You said insects were more advanced . . . ' I prompted.

'Yes, they accept their lives, which are shorter and perhaps more arduous. A female fruit-fly completes her whole lifecycle in ten days, whereas a turtle, for instance, can live for three hundred years.'

'I dread to think of what the turtle has been up to in his previous life to deserve such a long penance,' I said drily.

'Penance. Yes, that's a good way of putting it,' he said thoughtfully.

I groaned inwardly and was startled when the badger laughed out loud. 'All too much for you, is it?' he said. 'Well, that's understandable. But think about it: Why are certain creatures so repugnant to man? Why are they trodden on, mistreated or killed, or just plain reviled? Could these creatures have been so vile in their past lives that the malignancy lingers on? Is this their punishment for past crimes? The snake spends his life crawling on his belly, the spider is invariably crushed whenever he comes into contact with man. The worm is despised, the slug makes humans shudder. Even the poor old lobster is boiled alive. But their death comes as a blessing, a relief from their horrible existence. It's nature's way that their lives should be short, and man's instinct that makes him want to crush these creatures. It's not just abhorrence of them, you see, but compassion also, a desire to put an end to their misery. These creatures have paid their price.

'And there are many more, Fluke, many, *many* more creatures below the earth's surface. Beings that no human ever laid eyes on; bugs who live in fires near the earth's core. What evil have they done to earn such an existence? Have you ever wondered why humans think of hell as an inferno, why its direction is always "down there"? And why do we look skywards when we speak of "Heaven"? Do we have an instinct born in us about such things?

'Why do many fear death, while others welcome it? Do we already know it's only an enforced hibernation, that we live on in another form, that our wrongdoings have to be accounted for? No wonder those who have lived peaceful lives are less afraid.'

The badger paused at that point, either to regain his breath or to give me time to catch up with him.

'How do you explain ghosts, then? I know they exist, I've seen them – I keep seeing them,' I said. 'Why haven't they been born again as animals, or have they passed that stage? Is that the level we're reaching for? If it is, I'm not so sure I want it.'

'No, no. They haven't even reached our stage of development, I'm afraid, Fluke. They're closer to our world though than their previous one – that's why it's easier for us to see them – but they're lost, you see. That's why there's such an aura of sadness about them. Confused and lost. They find their way eventually with a little help. They get born again.'

Born again. The words struck me. Was this why my vision, the colours I could see, was so incredible? Was this why I could appreciate scents – the most delicate and the most pungent – so fully? Was it because I'd been born again yet still retained vague memories? *I had past senses to compare with the new!* A new-born baby sees freshly but quickly learns to adapt his vision, to mute colours, to organise shapes – he learns *not* to accept. That's why you're nearly blind at birth; it would be too much for you otherwise. Your brain has to sort things out first, then let you in on it gradually. My own sight was now nowhere as clear or un-prejudiced as it had been when I was a young pup. Nor was my hearing. My brain which had been born with the ability to appreciate my senses was now organising them so they were acceptable to it, so they no longer dazzled it as much as before.

I shook the train of thought from my head and said, 'But why can't others remember? Why aren't they the same as me?'

152

'I can't answer that, Fluke. You're different and I don't know why. Perhaps you're the first of a new development. An evolvement. I've met others similar, but none quite like you. Perhaps you are only a fluke after all. I wish I knew.'

'Aren't you the same as me? Wasn't Rumbo almost? And a rat we met once, he seemed like us.'

'Yes, we're a little like you. I suppose me more so than your friend Rumbo and the rat. But you're special, Fluke. I'm special too, but in a different way, as I told you: I'm here to help. Rumbo and the rat may have been similar, but I doubt they were the same. I think perhaps you're a kind of forerunner; everything may be about to go through a change.'

'But why do I only remember fragments? Why can't I remember it all?'

'You're not supposed to remember *anything*. Many creatures carry the characteristics of their past personalities, many may even have vague memories; but they don't think as you do, not in human terms. There's a struggle going on inside you – man versus canine – but I think it will eventually resolve itself. You'll either become a dog completely, or a balance between the two will be reached. I hope it's the latter – that could mean a development for all of us is taking place. But listen to me: you'll never be a man again physically in this life.'

Despair gripped me. What had I expected? That some day, by some miracle, I might return to my old body? That I would live a normal life again? I howled into the night and wept as never before.

Finally, and with no hope in my voice, I said to the badger, 'What do I do now? How can I live like this?'

He moved closer to me and spoke very quietly. 'You accept now. Accept you're a dog, accept you are a fluke – or perhaps not a fluke. You must live as a dog now.'

'But I have to know who I was!'

'No, it won't help you. Forget your past, your family – they're nothing to do with you now.'

'They need me!'

'There's nothing you can do!'

I rose to my feet and glowered down at him. 'You don't under-

153

stand. There's someone evil near them. They need protection from him. I think he killed me!'

The badger shook his head wearily. 'It doesn't matter, Fluke. You can't help any more. You *have* to forget your past, you might regret it if you go back.'

'No!' I growled. 'Maybe this is why I can remember, why I'm different. They need my help! It stayed with me when I died! I've got to go to them!'

I ran from the badger then, afraid he would make me stay, afraid to hear more, but when I was a safe distance away, I turned and called back.

'Who are you badger? What are you?'

There was no reply. And I could no longer see him in the darkness.

Sixteen

Pretty heavy stuff, right? A bit frightening? Well, it scared me. But do you see the sense of it? If there is this great goal we're all reaching for – call it perfection, happiness, ultimate peace of mind, whatever you like – then it seems right that it doesn't come easily; we have to earn it. I don't know why and I'm still not sure I believe it myself (and I'm a dog who was once a man), so I don't blame you for doubting. But, like I keep saying: keep an open mind.

I found myself in Edenbridge High Street a day or so later. I'm not sure just how long it took me to get there because, as you can imagine, my mind was in a turmoil after my meeting with the badger. I had to accept that, as a man, I was dead (if I were to believe the badger revelations), and there would be no return to normality for me. But if I were dead, then how did I die? Old age? Somehow, I doubted it. My wife seemed fairly young in my memories of her, and my daughter could have been no more than five or six. Illness? Possibly. Yet why did I feel so strongly against this mysterious man? Why was he so evil to me? Had he killed me?

I felt sure this was the answer, otherwise why should I feel such hate for him? I was determined to find the truth. First, though, I had to find my family.

The High Street was fairly busy with shoppers and delivery vans and the scene was vaguely familiar to me. I must have lived here, I told myself, or why else would I have been drawn to the

155

little town? It wouldn't click though, it just wouldn't click.

The shoppers must have been puzzled by the thoughtful-looking mongrel who paced up and down that street, peering up at passing faces, snooping into shop doorways. I ignored all enticements, for I had more serious things on my mind than playing games.

By late afternoon I was still no better off. I just couldn't remember clearly any of the shops, pubs or people, although everything appeared too frustratingly familiar! That old teaser hunger reminded me he was still around and had no intention of letting me off the hook just because *I* had problems. The shopkeepers shooed me away as soon as I put my sniffing nose through their doorways, and a sudden jaw-snapping thrust at an overloaded shopping-basket earned me a sharp smack on the snout and a lot of abuse.

Not wanting to cause a fuss (I didn't want to be picked up by the police since I needed to stay around that town until something happened to restore my memory) I left the main street and wandered on to what looked like a vast council estate. Then something did click, although it wasn't particularly helpful to me: many South Londoners had been moved down to Edenbridge over the last twenty or so years, away from their slums into modern estates surrounded by good countryside. Many had taken to their new environment, while others (like Lenny, the Guvnor's man) had still yearned for their old surroundings and spent much of their time to-ing and fro-ing from the two vastly different communities. I was conscious of all this because I'd obviously lived in the town and knew of its history, but where had I lived? On one of those estates? No, it didn't click; it didn't feel right.

I followed a couple of small boys home, much to their delight, and managed to scrounge a few scraps from their scolding but kind-hearted mother. The food wasn't much but enough to keep me going for a while, and to the boys' disappointment I scampered out of their back garden and towards the High Street again.

This time I drifted down all the side-streets on one side, then all the side-streets on the other, but nothing jarred that tiny trigger in my mind which I knew would unleash a flood of memories.

Night fell and so did my spirits. Nothing had happened. I'd felt so sure that when I reached the town it would be easy to find my home, familiar things would guide me to it, but it hadn't happened. I was still in the dark mentally, and now physically.

I wandered down to the very edge of the town, passing pubs, walking across a bridge, past a big garage, a hospital – and then the buildings ran out. There was only black countryside ahead. Utterly dejected, I entered the hospital grounds, found a quiet corner in the yard at the rear of the white single-storey building, and slept.

The smell of lovely cooking awoke me the following morning and I sniffed my way over to an open window from which it wafted. Rearing up on my hind legs, I rested my paws on the window-ledge. Unfortunately, the window was too high for me to see into the room beyond, but, sticking my nose into the air, I drank in the delicious smells, then cried out in appreciation. A huge round brown head suddenly appeared above and white teeth flashed a startled welcome at me. Reds and oranges shimmered in the woman's huge face as she grinned even more broadly.

'You hungry, fellah?' she chuckled, and I wagged my tail in anticipation. 'Now don' you go away,' she told me.

The beaming head disappeared then reappeared almost instantly, the smile now threatening to split the face in half. A thin, partly burnt slice of bacon was dangled before me.

'You get this down you, honey,' she said, dropping the hot finger of meat into my open mouth.

I spat the bacon out instantly as my throat was scorched then drooled saliva on the piping meat to cool it before wolfing it down.

'Good boy,' came the woman's voice from above, then another piece of bacon plopped on to the gravel beside me. This lasted for about as long as the first and I looked up hopefully, tongue hanging out.

'You's a greedy dog!' said the coloured (multicoloured) woman, laughing. 'O.K., I get you one more, then you scat – you get me into trouble!'

The promised third slice appeared and disappeared almost as quickly, and I looked up for more. Still chuckling, the woman waggled her index finger at me and then closed the window as a final word.

It wasn't a bad start to the day and my spirits rose as I trotted round to the hospital's main entrance. Hot food in my belly and a day for discovery ahead of me! Perhaps life (or death) wasn't so bad after all. Dogs are born optimists, as I said.

I reached the entrance and turned left, heading towards the High Street again, sure it was my only chance of finding someone or something I knew.

Without thinking, I wandered into the road and screamed with fright as a green monster roared down on me. The single-decker bus screeched to a halt as I scurried to the other side of the road, tail between my legs and hair on end, and the driver hurled abuse at me, thumping his horn angrily. I cowered in a hedge and rolled my eyes at him, and with a final threatening gesture he threw his vehicle into gear again and slowly moved off.

As the row of windows went by, accusing faces glared down at me while others shook in pity. And one small pair of eyes locked into mine and held my gaze until the progress of the bus no longer allowed them to. Even then, the little girl's head craned round and pushed itself against the glass so I was visible for as long as possible.

Only when the bus had disappeared over the hump-backed bridge did I realise just whom I had been looking at and had been returning my stare. It was my daughter, Gillian, only I called her Polly because I preferred the name! I had been right! Edenbridge was my hometown! I had found them!

But I hadn't found them. The bus was gone and no memories came flooding back. I remembered the names, the minor disagreement over my daughter's, but that was all. I waited for the visions to appear, sure they would, but they didn't.

I groaned in disappointment and longing, then set off after the bus, determined to catch it, refusing to throw away such a chance encounter. As I mounted the hump of the bridge I saw the bus at a stop in the distance. Barking in my eagerness, I increased my speed and hurtled down that High Street like a bullet from a gun.

It was no use, though; the bus lurched forward and continued its journey down the long road. I watched it getting smaller and smaller and my legs grew wearier and wearier until I came to a panting halt.

It was hopeless. The bus – and my child – had got away.

Two more days of anguished searching went by – searching of the town and searching of my mind – both of which proved fruitless. I had eaten regularly at the hospital, having my breakfast and evening meal there thanks to the generosity of the coloured cook, and had spent the rest of the time looking through the town and its outer fringes, but all to no avail. Then on the third day, which must have been a Saturday judging by the amount of shoppers there were around, I struck lucky.

I had been wandering up and down the High Street, trying to make myself as inconspicuous as possible (a few people had already tried to catch me now I was becoming a familiar sight around the shops), and had glanced down the small side-turning which led to the car park at the rear of the shops. There I caught a glimpse of a small familiar figure skipping alongside the much taller figure of a woman. They disappeared around a corner but I knew instantly who they were. My heart tried to escape through my throat and my knees suddenly went wobbly.

'Carol!' I gurgled. 'Carol! Polly! Wait for me! Stay there!'

The shoppers must have thought they had a mad dog amongst them, for they all froze at the sound of my barking and stared in amazement as I staggered into the small side-turning. It was like a bad dream, for the shock had turned my legs to jelly and they refused to function properly. I took a grip of myself, realising this was a chance I just could not afford to miss, and willed the power to flow through my quakey limbs. It did, but I had lost valuable seconds. I set off in pursuit of the two figures, mother and daughter, my wife and my child, and was just in time to see them climbing into a green Renault.

'Carol! Stop! It's me!'

They turned and looked in my direction, surprise then fear showing in their faces.

'Quick, Gillian,' I heard my wife say, 'get in the car and close the door!'

'No, Carol! It's me! Don't you know me?'

I was soon across the car park and yapping around the Renault, frantic for my wife to recognise me.

They both stared down at me, their fright obvious. I didn't have the sense to calm down, my emotions were running too high. Carol rolled down the window on her side and flapped a hand at me. 'Shoo, go away! Bad dog!'

'Carol, for Christ's sake, it's me – Nigel! (Nigel? I remembered that was my previous name; I think I preferred Horace.)

'Mummy, it's the poor doggy I told you about, the one that nearly got run over,' I heard my daughter say.

Then I did a quick double-take. Was this my daughter? She seemed much older than I remembered; at least two or three years older. But the woman *was* Carol, and she had called the girl Gillian. Of course it was my daughter!

I leapt up at the side of the car and pushed my nose against the bottom of the half-open window.

'Polly, it's your daddy! Don't you remember me, Polly?' I pleaded.

Carol smacked me on the top of the head, not viciously but defensively. Then the car's engine roared into life, the gears clunked, and the vehicle began slowly to move away.

'No!' I screamed. 'Don't leave me, Carol! Please don't leave me!'

I ran alongside the car, dangerously close, but it gathered speed and soon outpaced me. I was sobbing by now, seeing them slip through my paws like this, knowing I could never match their speed, realising they were driving from my life again. I felt like throwing myself beneath the wheels to make them stop, but common sense and my old chum, cowardice, prevented me from doing so.

'Come back, come back, come back!'

But they wouldn't.

I saw Polly's wide-eyed face as the car twisted its way round the winding road that led from the car park to the outskirts of the town, and willed her to make her mother stop the car; but it was no use, they sped away.

Many onlookers were regarding me rather nervously by now and I had the good judgement to make myself scarce before I was reported. I took off after the Renault and, as I ran, memories began to pour into me.

Soon, I remembered where I had lived.

Seventeen

Marsh Green is a tiny, one-street village just outside Edenbridge. It has a church at one end and a pub at the other, one general store in the middle and a few houses on either side. There are other houses hidden away at the back of these, one of which I stood gazing at now.

I knew this was where my wife and daughter lived — where I had once lived. My name had been Nigel Nettle (yes, I'm afraid so) and I had originally come from Tonbridge, Kent. As a boy, I'd spent a lot of time working for local farmers (hence my knowledge of the countryside and animals), but careerwise I'd turned to — of all things — plastics. I'd managed to set up a small factory in Edenbridge on the industrial estate leading to the town and had specialised in flexible packaging, branching out into other areas as the firm prospered and grew. Speaking as a dog, it all seemed very boring, but I suppose at the time the company meant a lot to me. We had moved to Marsh Green to be near the business, and I had found myself taking more and more trips up to London for business reasons (which is why the route was so familiar).

As far as I could remember, we'd been very happy: my love for Carol had never diminished with time, only grown more comfortable; Polly (Gillian) was a delight, our home was a dream, and the business was expanding rapidly. So what had happened? I had died, that's what.

How, and when (Polly seemed so much older than I remembered) I had yet to find out; but I was even more convinced my death was connected with the mysterious man who floated into view so often, yet eluded me before recognition. If he were still a threat to my family (and *that* thought still clung to me), and if he had had something to do with my death (something told me he had been the *cause* of it), then I would find a way of dealing with him. Right now, though, I just wanted to be with Carol and Polly.

It was mid-afternoon, I think, and the sun was hidden behind heavy clouds. I was at the bottom of an unmade road and staring at the detached house before me. The walls of the ground floor were constructed of red brick, while the upper floor's surface was covered with red clay tiles; the doors and window-frames were painted white. A feeling of warmth spread through me and I swallowed hard.

I had to steady myself, it was no good acting the way I had in the town; they would only become frightened again. Keep yourself under control, I told myself, act like a normal dog; there'll be plenty of time to let them know who you really are once they've got used to you.

Pushing the latch of the garden gate down with a paw, I nudged my way in and trotted up the path, keeping a firm rein on trembling body and quaking nerves. I reached the front door and scratched at its surface with a paw.

Nothing happened. I tried again and still nothing happened. I knew they were in, because the Renault stood in the open garage to my left.

I woofed, quietly at first, then louder. 'Carol!' I called out. 'It's me, Carol, open the door!'

I heard footsteps inside, footsteps coming along the hall towards me. With a great effort of will, I stopped my barking and waited. The door opened slightly and a solitary eye peered through the two-inch crack.

'Mummy, it's that dog again!' Polly cried out. The crack shrunk to an inch, the eye now regarding me with both excitement and trepidation.

More footsteps sounded down the hallway, then Carol's eye appeared above my daughter's. She looked at me in amazement.

'How did *you* get here?' she said.

'I remembered where we lived, Carol. I couldn't follow the car,

163

but I remembered. It didn't take long!' I was finding it hard to contain myself.

'Scat! Go away now, there's a good dog,' Carol urged.

I whimpered. I didn't want to go away; I'd only just found them.

'Oh Mummy, I think he's hungry,' Polly said.

'It might be dangerous, dear. We can't take chances.'

'Please,' I wailed, giving them my most beseeching look. 'I need you. Don't turn me away.'

'Look, Mummy, I think he's crying!'

And I was. Tears rolled down my cheeks.

'That's impossible,' Carol said. 'Dogs don't cry.'

But they do. In fact, I wasn't just crying, I was blubbering.

'Let him come in, please, Mummy. I'm sure he doesn't mean us any harm,' Polly pleaded.

Carol looked doubtful. 'I don't know. It doesn't look very dangerous, but you never know with dogs. They're a bit unpredictable.'

I was really snivelling by now and looking as pitiful as I could. The hardest heart would have melted and I knew my wife's heart was by no means hard.

'All right then, let it in,' she said with a sigh.

The door flew open and I flew in, crying and laughing at the same time, kissing and licking hands and legs. They were startled at first and leapt back in alarm, but soon realised I was only being friendly. 'He's lovely, Mummy!' Polly cried, and knelt on both knees to cuddle me. Fear showed on Carol's face for a second but she relaxed as I smothered Polly's face with wet kisses. It's impossible to tell you how wonderful that moment was — even now it gives me a choking feeling — but if parts of your lives closed in episodes as in a book, then that would have been the end of a chapter. Maybe the end of the book.

My wife joined my daughter on the floor, ruffling my hair with a gentle hand, and I made the mistake of trying to take her in my arms and kiss her on the lips. She screamed in horrified glee and we became a struggling heap of squirming, giggling bodies on the hallway carpet. Polly tried to pull me off and her fingers dug into my ribs, making me shriek with laughter. The harsh tickling continued when she realised she had found my vulnerable spot. The fun stopped when the first sprinkle of water jetted from me (I tried hard but I've never been on the best of terms with my bladder) and Carol leapt to her feet, caught hold of my collar and dragged me towards the door.

I found myself outside on the path again, and to convince my wife I was really quite clean I went through the exaggerated pantomime of cocking a leg (an art in itself) and sprinkling her flowerbed. She wasn't too pleased about the flowers, but understood I was trying to prove something. I waited patiently, beaming up at her, tail wagging itself into a blur, wanting desperately to hug her and tell her I still loved her, until she invited me back into the house.

'Thank you!' I barked, and shot past her legs down the hallway.

Polly chased after me, her laughter beautiful to my ears. I skidded to a halt when I reached the kitchen and my eyes drank in the room, the memories returning like old friends from an outing: the huge old black fireplace with its iron oven, a relic of the past which we decided to preserve; the round pine table, deliberately scored and scratched with initials, noughts and crosses, I LOVE YOUs and HAPPY BIRTHDAYs, and any messages we cared to mark for posterity; the antique clock which always informed us the time was a quarter to four, but did so in such an elegant way; the blue-and-yellow vase on the window-sill that looked as if it had been made up from a jigsaw, the result of my patiently piecing it together after Polly had knocked it on to the floor in her 'just-about-walking' days. There were new items around the kitchen, of course, but these seemed alien, an intrusion upon a memory. I sighed, ready to burst into tears again, but a hand grabbed my collar and interrupted my nostalgia.

'Let's just see who you belong to,' Carol said, tugging the nameplate round into view. 'Fluke? Is that your name?'

Polly cupped a hand to her mouth and tittered.

'No address? Nobody wants you, do they?' Carol said, shaking her head.

I shook my own head in agreement.

'Can we keep him?' Polly said excitedly.

'No,' was Carol's firm reply. 'We'll take it to the police station tomorrow and see if it's been reported missing.'

'But can we keep him if no one wants him?'

'I don't know, we'll have to ask Uncle Reg.'

Uncle Reg? Who was he?

Polly seemed pleased enough with that and began to run her fingers down my back. 'Can we feed Fluke, Mummy? I'm sure he's very hungry.'

'Let's see what we've got for it, then.'

Please call me him, or he, Carol, not *it*. I'm not an *it*. I prefer Fluke to *it*. I prefer *Horace* to *it*.

Carol went to a freezer, a new item in the kitchen, and looked thoughtfully into it. 'I'm sure you'd like a leg of lamb or some nice juicy steak, wouldn't you, Fluke?'

I nodded, licking my lips in anticipation, but she closed the freezer and said to Polly, 'Run down to the shop and buy a tin of dogfood. That should keep him happy until tomorrow.'

'Can I take Fluke with me, Mummy?' Polly jumped up and down at the prospect and I began to get excited at her excitement.

'All right, but make sure he doesn't run out into the main road.'

So off we set, my daughter and I, girl and dog, down the lane that led to the main road and the village's only shop. We played as we went and for a while I forgot I was Polly's father and became her companion. I stayed close to her skipping feet, occasionally jumping up to pull at her cardigan, licking her face anxiously once when she tripped and fell. I tried to lick her grazed knees clean, but she pushed me away and wagged a reprimanding finger. While she was buying my dinner in the grocery I stayed on my best behaviour, refusing to be tempted by the pile of within-easy-reach packets of potato crisps, 'all flavours'. We raced back down the lane and I let her beat me for most of the way, hiding behind a tree when she reached the garden gate. She looked around, bewildered, and called out my name; I remained hidden, snickering into the long grass at the base of the tree. I heard footsteps coming back down the lane and, when she drew level with my hiding-place, raced around the other side, scooting towards the gate. Polly caught sight of me and gave chase, but I was an easy winner.

She reached me, giggling and breathless, and threw her arms around my neck, squeezing me tight.

We went into the house – my home – and Polly told Carol everything that had happened. Half the tin of dogfood was poured on to a plate and placed on the floor, together with a dish full of water. I buried my nose in the meat and cleared the plate. Then I cleared the dish. Then I begged for more. And more I got.

Everything was rosy. I was home, I was with my family. I had food in my belly and hope in my heart. I'd find a way of letting them know who I was, and if I couldn't . . . well, did it matter *that* much? As long as I was with them, there to protect them, there to keep the mysterious stranger at bay, my true identity wasn't that important. I wasn't worried about the police station tomorrow, for there'd be no one to claim me, and I was sure I could ingratiate myself enough for them to want to keep me. Yes, everything was rosy.

And you know how things have a habit of turning nasty for me just at their rosiest.

We'd settled down for the night (I thought). Polly was upstairs in bed, Carol was relaxed on the settee, her legs tucked up beneath her as she watched television, and I lay sprawled on the floor below her, my eyes never leaving hers. Occasionally, she would look down at me and smile, and I would smile back, breathing deep sighs of contentment. Several times I tried to tell her who I was, but she didn't seem to understand, telling me to stop grizzling. I gave up in the end and succumbed to the tiredness that had crept up on me. I couldn't sleep – I was too happy for that – but I rested and studied my wife's features with adoring eyes.

She'd aged slightly, lines at the corners of her eyes and at the base of her neck where there'd been no lines before. There was a sadness about her, but it was a well-hidden inner sadness, one you had to sense rather than see; it was obvious to me why it was there.

I wondered how she had coped without me, how Polly had

accepted my death. I wondered about my own acceptance of the badger's pronouncement that I certainly was dead as a man. The lounge still contained all the cosiness I remembered so well, but the atmosphere of the whole house was very different now. Part of its personality had gone, and that was me. It's people who create atmosphere, not wood or brick, nor accessories – they only create surroundings.

I had looked around for photographs, hoping to catch a glimpse of my past image, but to my surprise had found none on display. I racked my brain to remember if ever there had been any framed photographs of myself around, but as usually happens whenever I try consciously to remember, my mind became a blank. Perhaps they had been too painful a reminder to Carol and Polly and had been put away somewhere to be taken out only when they could cope.

Whether my plastics business had been sold or was still running I had no way of knowing, but I was relieved to see my family seemed to be under no great hardship. Various household items confirmed this: the freezer in the kitchen, the new television set here in the lounge, various odd items of furniture scattered about the house.

Carol was still as attractive as ever, despite the telltale lines; she'd never been what you might call beautiful, but her face possessed a quality that made it seem so. Her body was still an inch away from plumpness all round, as it always had been, her legs long and gracefully curved. Ironically, for the first time as a dog, I felt physical feeling stir, a hunger aroused. I wanted my wife, but she was a woman and I was a dog.

I quickly turned my thoughts towards Polly. How she'd grown! She'd lost her baby chubbiness but retained her prettiness, fair skin and darkening hair emphasising her small, delicately featured face. I was surprised and strangely moved to see her don brown-rimmed spectacles to watch television earlier on in the evening; it seemed to make her even more vulnerable somehow. I was pleased with her; she'd grown into a gentle child, with none of the petulance or awkwardness so many of her age seemed to have. And there was a special closeness between her and her mother, perhaps a closeness born out of mutual loss.

As I had noticed before, she appeared to be about seven or eight, and I pondered over the question of how long I had been dead.

Outside, the sky had dulled as night bullied its way in, and a chill had crept into the air with it, an agitator urging the night on. Carol switched on one of those long, sleek electric fires (another new item, for we'd always insisted on open fires in the past – logs and coal and flames – but maybe that romanticism had gone with me) and settled back on the settee. Headlights suddenly brightened up the room and I heard a car crunching its way down the gravelly lane. It stopped outside and the engine purred on while gates grated their way open. Carol craned her head around and looked towards the window, then turned her attention back towards the television, tidying her hair with deft fingers and smoothing her skirt over her thighs. The car became mobile again, the glare from its lights swinging around the room and then vanishing. The engine stopped, a car door slammed, and a shadowy figure walked past the window rattling fingers against the glass as it did so.

My head jerked up and I growled menacingly, following the shadow until it had gone from view.

'Shhh, Fluke! Settle down.' Carol reached forward and patted the top of my head.

I heard a key going into its latch, then footsteps in the hallway. I was on my feet now. Carol grabbed my collar, concern showing on her face. My body stiffened as the door of the lounge began to open.

'Hello . . .' a man's voice began to say, and he entered the room, a smile on his face.

I broke loose from Carol's grip and went for him, a roar of rage and hate tearing itself from me. I recognised him.

It was the man who had killed me!

Eighteen

I leapt up, my teeth seeking his throat, but the man managed to get an arm between us. It was better than nothing so I sank my teeth into that instead.

Carol was screaming, but I paid her no heed; I wouldn't let this assassin anywhere near her. He cried out at the sudden pain and grabbed at my hair with his other hand; we fell back against the door jamb and slid to the floor. My attack was ferocious for my hate was strong, and I could smell the fear in him. I relished it.

Hands grabbed me from behind and I realised Carol was trying to tug me away, obviously afraid I would kill the man. I hung on; she didn't understand the danger she was in.

For a few snap seconds I found myself eye-to-eye with him and his face seemed so familiar. And strangely – perhaps I imagined it – there seemed to be some recognition in his eyes too. The moment soon passed and we became a frenzied heap again. Carol had her arms around my throat and was squeezing and pulling at the same time; my victim had his free hand around my nose, fingers curled into my upper jaw, and was trying to prise my grip loose. Their combined strength had its effect: I was forced to let go.

Instantly, the man slammed me in my under-belly with a clenched fist and I yelped at the pain, choking and trying to draw in breath immediately afterwards. I went straight back into the attack, but he'd had a chance to close both hands around my jaws, clamping my mouth tightly shut. I tried to rake him with my nails, but they had little effect against the suit he was wearing.

Pushing myself into him was no use either; Carol's restraining arms around my neck held me back. I called out to her to let me go, but all that emerged from my clenched jaws was a muted growling noise.

'Hang on to it, Carol!' the man gasped. 'Let's get it out the door!'

Keeping one hand tight around my mouth, he grabbed my collar between Carol's arms and began to drag me into the hall. Carol helped by releasing one arm from my neck and grasping my tail. They propelled me forward and tears of frustration formed in my eyes. Why was Carol helping him?

As I was dragged towards the front door, I caught a glimpse of Polly at the top of the stairs, tears streaming down her face.

'Stay there!' Carol called out when she, too, saw her. 'Don't come down!'

'What are you doing with Fluke, Mummy?' she wailed. 'Where are you taking him?'

'It's all right, Gillian,' the man answered her between grunts. 'We've got to get it outside.'

'Why, why? What's he done?'

They ignored her for, realising I was losing, I had become frantic. I squirmed my body, twisting my neck, dug my paws into the carpet. It was no use, they were too strong.

When we reached the front door he told Carol to open it, afraid to let go himself. She did and I felt the breeze rush in and ruffle my hair. With one last desperate effort I wrenched my head free and cried out, 'Carol, it's me, Nigel! I've come back to you! Don't let him do this to me!'

But of course all she heard was a mad dog barking.

I managed to tear the sleeve of the man's coat and draw blood from his wrist before being thrust out and having the door slammed in my face.

I jumped up and down outside, throwing myself at the door and howling. Carol's voice came to me through the wood; she was trying to soothe Polly. Then I heard the man's voice. The words 'mad dog' and 'attacker' reached my ears and I realised he was speaking to someone on the phone.

'No! Don't let him, Carol! Please, it's me!' I knew he was calling the police.

And sure enough, not more than five minutes later, headlights appeared at the end of the lane and a car bumped its way towards the house. I was underneath the ground floor window by now, running backwards and forwards, screaming and ranting, while Carol, Polly and the man watched me, white-faced. To my dismay, the man had his arms around both Carol's and Polly's shoulders.

The little blue-and-white Panda car lurched to a halt and doors flew open as though it had suddenly sprouted butterfly wings. Two dark figures leapt from it, one carrying a long pole with a loop attached to it. I knew what *that* was for and decided not to give them a chance to use it. I fled into the night; but not too far into it.

Later when the police had given up thrashing around in the dark in search of me, I crept back. I'd heard voices coming from the house, car doors slam, an engine start, then tyres crunching their way back down the lane. No doubt they'd be back tomorrow to give the area a thorough going over in the daylight, but for tonight I knew I'd be safe. I'd wait for the man to come out of the house and then I'd do my best to follow him – or maybe get him there and then. No, that would be foolish – it would only frighten Carol and Polly again, and Carol would probably call the police back. Besides, the man was a little too strong for me. That would be the best bet: follow him somehow – maybe I could even track his car's scent (even cars have their own distinct smell) – then attack him, the element of surprise on my side. It was a harebrained scheme, but then I was a pretty hare-brained dog. So I settled down to wait. And I waited. And waited.

The shock of it hit me a few hours later: he wasn't coming out that night. His car was still in the drive so I knew he hadn't already left, and there would have been no reason for him to have gone with the police. He was staying the night!

How could you, Carol? All right, I'd obviously been cold in my grave at least a couple of years, but how could you with him?

172

The man who had murdered me? How could you with anyone after all we'd shared? Had it meant so little that you'd forget so soon?

My howl filled the night and seconds later curtains moved in the bedroom window. My bedroom window!

How could such evil exist? He's killed me, then taken my wife! He'd pay – oh, I'd make him pay!

I ran from the house then, unable to bear the pain of looking at it, imagining what was going on inside. I crashed around in the dark, frightening night creatures, disturbing those who were sleeping, and finally fell limp and weeping into a hollow covered with brambles. There I stayed till dawn.

Nineteen

Have patience now, my story's nearly done.

Do you still disbelieve all I've told you? I don't blame you –
I'm not sure I believe it myself. Maybe I'm a dog who's just had
hallucinations. How is it you understand me, though? You *do*
understand me, don't you?

How's the pain? You'll forget it later; memories of pain are
always insubstantial unless you actually *feel* the pain again.
How's the fear? Are you less afraid now, or more afraid? Anyway,
let me go on: you're not going anywhere, and I've got all the
time in the world. Where was I? Oh yes ...

Dawn found me, full of self-pity again, confused and disappointed. But, as I keep telling you, dogs are born optimists; I
decided to be constructive about my plight. First I would find
out a little more about myself – like exactly when I died – and
then the circumstances of my death. The first would be easy, for
I had a good idea of where I would find myself. You see, now
I was in familiar surroundings, memories had started to soak
through. Well, perhaps not memories, but – how can I put it? –
recognitions were soaking through. I was on home ground. I
knew where I was. Hopefully, memories of events would soon
follow.

The second part – the circumstances of my death – was more
difficult, and because I felt familiar places would begin to open
memory valves, a visit to my plastics factory might help.

First, though: When did I die?

The graveyard was easy to find, since I knew the location of the dominating church (although the inside wasn't too familiar to me). What was hard to locate, was my own grave. Reading had become difficult by now and many of these gravestones were poorly marked anyway. I found mine after two hours of squinting and concentrating, and was pleased to see it was still neat and tidy in appearance. I suppose to you it would seem a macabre kind of search, but I promise you, being dead is the most natural thing in the world, and it disturbed me not in the least to be mooching around for my own epitaph.

A small white cross marked my resting-place, and neatly inscribed on it were these words: 'NIGEL CLAIREMOUNT' – I'm not kidding – 'NETTLE. BELOVED HUSBAND OF CAROL, BELOVED FATHER OF GILLIAN. BORN 1943 – DIED 1975.' I'd died at the age of thirty-two, so it seemed unlikely it was from natural causes. Below this, two more words were carved out in the stone, and these made my eyes mist up. These simply said: 'NEVER FORGOTTEN.'

Oh yes? I thought bitterly.

The plastics factory was easy to locate too. In fact, as I trotted through the town, I began to remember the shops, the little restaurants, and the pubs. How I would have loved to have gone in and ordered a pint! I realised it was now Sunday, for the High Street was quiet and in the distance I could hear church bells start their guilt-provoking ringing. It was still early morning, but the thought that the pubs would not be open for a few hours yet did not lessen their attraction; I remembered I had always enjoyed my Sunday lunchtime drink.

The sight of the one-floor factory itself, almost a mile beyond the town, stirred up old feelings, a mixture of pride, excitement and anxiety. It was small, but modern and compact, and I could see a fairly substantial extension had recently been added. A long sign, itself made of plastic and which I knew lit up at night, stretching along the face of the building, read: 'NETTLE & NEWMAN – ADVANCED PLASTICS LTD.'

Nettle & Newman, I pondered. Newman? Who was Newman . . . ? Yes, you've guessed it. My killer had been my partner.

175

It all began to take shape, all began to fall into place; and the thing that hurt most of all was that he wasn't content just to take my business — he'd taken my wife too. I remembered him clearly now, his face — his person — clearly formed in my mind. We had started the business together, built it up from nothing, shared our failures, rejoiced together in our successes. He had the shrewder business brain (although he could be rash), but I had the greater knowledge — an almost instinctive knowledge — of plastics. It seems crazy now, a silly thing to be proud of, but proud I had been of that knowledge. Plastics! You can't even eat them! We had been good partners for a time, almost like brothers, respecting each other's particular flair. It was often I, though, as smart as my partner had been, who had a hunch on business matters and, as I remember, could be very stubborn if I considered a certain direction was the right or wrong one to take. I believe it was this stubbornness which began to lead to our disagreements.

The facts of the disputes hadn't swung into focus yet, but the image of heated arguments in the latter days of our partnership clung heavily to my mind. It had seemed our disagreement would lead to the breaking up of the company at one time, but then what had happened?

Obviously I'd been murdered.

Newman. Reginald Newman. Uncle Reg! That's what Carol had said to Polly when she'd asked about keeping me — 'Wait till Uncle Reg gets home'. Something like that! The creep had really crept in! Had I been aware of his intentions before I'd died? Was that why I was different? Was I like one of those unfortunate ghosts I'd seen, tied to their past existence because of some grievance, some undone thing holding them? Had I been allowed (or had my own natural stubbornness caused it?) to keep old memories in order to set things right?

I stood erect, vengeful, defiant of the odds. I would protect my own. (There's nothing worse than an idiot ennobled by revenge.)

The factory was closed for the day, but I sniffed around the outside wondering about the new extension built on to the back of the building. Business must have been good since my death.

After a while I got bored. Strange to think that an interest which had been a large part of my life should seem so uninteresting, so trivial, but I'm afraid after my initial stirring of emotions it all seemed very dull. I went off and chased some rabbits in a nearby field.

I returned to my home later on in the day and was surprised to find it empty. The car was gone from the drive and no noises came from the house. It seemed an empty shell now, just like the factory; they had both lost their meaning. Without their occupants, without my direct involvement, they were just bricks and mortar. I don't remember being conscious of this sudden impersonal attitude in me at the time, and it's only now, in times of almost complete lucidity, that I'm aware of the changes which have taken place in my personality over the years.

Starvation became my biggest concern – at least, the prevention of it – so I trotted back to the main road through the village and the ever-open grocery store. A lightning raid on the 'all-flavours' secured me a small lunch although a hasty departure from Marsh Green.

I took to the open fields when a blue-and-white patrol car slowed down and a plod stuck his head out of the window and called enticingly to me. After my attack on dear Reggie the night before, I knew the local police would be keeping a sharp lookout for me; you're not allowed to attack a member of the public unless you've been trained to do so.

A romp with a flock of longwools (sheep to you) passed a joyful hour for me until a ferocious collie appeared on the scene and chased me off. The derision from the sheep at my hasty retreat irritated me, but I saw there was no reasoning with their canine guardian: he was too subservient to man.

A cool drink in a busy little stream, a nibble at a clump of shaggy inkcaps – edible mushrooms – and a doze in the long grass filled out the rest of the afternoon.

I awoke refreshed and single-minded. I returned to the factory and began my vigil.

He showed up early next morning, much earlier than any of

our – I mean his – employees. I was tucking into a young rabbit I'd found sleepy-eyed in the nearby field (sorry, but canine instinct was taking over more and more – I was quite proud of my kill, actually), when the sound of his car interrupted me. I crouched low, even though I was well hidden in the hedge dividing field from factory, and growled in a menacing, dog-like way. The sun was already strong and his feet disturbed fine sandy dust from the asphalt as he stepped from the car.

The muscles in my shoulder bunched as I readied myself to attack. I wasn't sure what I could do against a man, but hate left little room for logic. Just as I was about to launch myself forward, another car drew in from the main road and parked itself alongside Newman's. A chubby grey-suited man waved at Newman as he emerged from the car. The face was familiar, but it was only when an image of the chubby man in a white smock flashed into my mind that I remembered him to be the technical manager. A good man, a little unimaginative, but conscientious and hard-working enough to make up for it.

'Scorcher again today, Mr Newman,' he said, smiling at the foe.

'No doubt of it. Same as yesterday, I reckon,' Newman replied, pulling a briefcase from the passenger seat of his car.

'You look as if you caught some of it,' the manager replied. 'In the garden, were you, yesterday?'

'Nope. Decided to get away from it all and take Carol and Gillian down to the coast.'

'I bet they appreciated that.'

Newman gave a short laugh. 'Yes, I've spent too many weekends going over paperwork lately. No fun for the wife.'

The manager nodded as he waited for Newman to open the office entrance to the factory. 'How is she now?' I heard him say.

'Oh . . . much better. Still misses him, of course, even after all this time, but then we all do. Let's go over this week's schedule while it's still quiet . . . ' Their voices took on a hollow sound as they entered the building and the door closing cut them off completely.

Wife? She's married him? I was bewildered. And hurt even more. He'd really got everything!

My fury seethed and boiled throughout the day, but I stayed well hidden as the factory buzzed into activity and became a living thing. A coldness finally took over me as I waited in the shade of the hedge: I would bide my time, wait for the right moment.

Newman emerged again around midday, jacket over his arm, tie undone. There were too many factory workers around, sitting in the shade with their backs against the building, munching sandwiches, others lounging shirtless under the full blast of the sun; I stayed hidden. He climbed into his car, wound down a window, and drove off into the main road.

I gritted my teeth with frustration. I could wait, though.

The murderer returned about an hour later, but again, there was nothing I could do – still too much activity.

I slept and evening came. The workers – many of whom I now recognised – left the building, relieved to escape its exhausting heat. The office staff, consisting of two girls and an administrator, followed shortly after, and the chubby technical manager an hour after that. Newman worked on.

A light went on when dusk began to set in and I knew it came from our – his – office. I crept from my hiding-place and padded over to the building, gazing up at the window. I stood on my hind legs and rested my front legs against the brickwork, but even though I craned my neck till the tendons stood out I could not see into the office. The fluorescent light in the ceiling was visible, but nothing else.

I dropped to all fours and did a quick tour of the building looking for any openings. There were none.

As I completed the circuit, I saw the lone car standing where he had parked it face on to the building. And as I approached, I noticed the window on the driver's side had been left open. It had been a hot day.

The thing to do was obvious: the means to do it a little more difficult. It took four painful attempts to get the front portion of my body through that opening, and then a lot of back leg scrabbling and elbow heaving to get my tender belly over the sill.

I finally piled over on to the driver's seat and lay there panting, waiting for the pain from my scraped underside to recede. Then I slid through the gap between the front seats into the back and hid there in the dark cavity on the floor, my body trembling all over.

It was at least an hour before Newman decided he'd had enough work for one day and left the office. My ears pricked up at the sound of the front door being locked and I slunk low when the car door jerked open and a briefcase came flying through on to the passenger seat. The car rocked as he climbed in and I did my best to contain my eagerness to get at him. He started the engine, clicking the light switch, and reversed the car from its parking space. A hand fell over the back seat as he reversed and the temptation to bite his fingers off was almost overpowering, but I needed something more than my own strength if I were to claim retribution.

I needed his car's speed.

He swung into the main road and sped towards the town. He had to pass through Edenbridge to reach Marsh Green and, as town and village were not too far apart, I knew I hadn't too long to make my move. There was a long straight stretch of road leading from the town before it curved to the left towards Hartfield, and a smaller road to Marsh Green joining it from the right on its apex. Most cars speeded up on the clear stretch before the bend and it seemed likely he would do the same, for the road would be fairly empty at that time of night. That was where I would go into action – even if it meant being killed myself. I'd died before; it would be easy to do so again. After all, what did I have to lose? A dog's life?

The thought of what this evil man had reduced me to made the blood rush through me again, and the anger beat against my chest. A low rumbling started way down in my throat and began to rise, molten lava full of hate, seeking an opening, gushing up the hot passage of my throat and finally bursting through to the surface with a scream, an eruption of violence.

I saw the fear in his face as he looked back over his shoulder, his eyes wide and white-filled, forgetting to take his foot off the accelerator, the car speeding on unguided. I had time to see the bend was almost upon us before I lunged forward and bit into his cheek.

He went forward, trying to avoid my slashing teeth, but I went with him, catching and tearing his ear. He screeched and I screeched and the car screeched. And we all went crashing off the road together.

My body hurtled through the windscreen and suddenly I was bathed in a blinding whiteness as I skimmed along the bonnet and into the beam of the headlights. For a split second, lasting for at least a year, I felt as if I were floating in an incandescent womb; until darkness and pain hit me as one.

Then I remembered all and knew I'd been so very, very wrong.

Twenty

Reg Newman had been a true friend. Even after my death.

The realisation hit me along with the pain as I lay there stunned and breathless in the dusty lane – the small lane rutted and stone-filled, which ran directly on from the main road, used only by residents who lived further down its length. We'd been lucky: instead of running into the trees lining the sides of the bend, the car had plunged straight ahead into the lane, the rough bank at one side bringing it to a gut-wrenching halt.

The fragments joined; pieces merged, the jigsaw made a whole. I knew why the bad memories of Reg had lingered on after death, why my very death had confused and distorted those memories. I saw how the stupidities of life could warp the senses in the afterlife, unsettle a soul's peace. I lay there and let my mind welcome the memories, ashamed and relieved at the same time. I saw the images of my ex-partner had been only vague because he'd been connected with my death and part of me had wanted to forget why and how I had died. Because I had only myself to blame.

We'd had many disagreements in our partnership, but one or other of us had usually given way out of mutual respect for the other's special qualities: Reg's business acumen or my knowledge of plastics. Only this time it had been different. This time neither of us was prepared to back down.

The argument was one we were bound to reach at some time in our growth: level out or expand. I was for levelling out, maintaining our position in soft plastics, improving and diversifying only in certain areas. Reg was for expanding, going for hard plastics, investigating the qualities of polypropylene in this area. He maintained that eventually glass would be a thing of the past, that it would be replaced by the more durable plastic, first in the container market, then in most other areas where glass was now used. Polypropylene seemed to possess most of the qualities needed: clarity, strength, the ability to withstand a variety of temperatures, and it was durable to most conditions.

We were using polythylene mainly at that time for flexible packaging such as carrier-bags, frozen food pouches and containers for garden feed produce; to change from this to hard plastics would have meant a huge investment. While I agreed with my partner about the future of plastics, I argued we were not ready to venture into that field just yet. The company would need new extruders for the raw materials to be softened and moulded, the factory itself enlarged or a complete move made to a bigger site. In addition new technical staff and engineers would be required, and transport costs would rocket because of the larger delivery bulk. It would take an investment of not less than one and a half million pounds to bring it off. And that would mean bringing in new partners, perhaps even merging with another company. The business, I argued, was fine as it was; let other companies pave the way into these new areas. It would be foolish for us to take expansion risks so soon after the oil crisis anyway. If it happened again, or if there were serious delays in bringing home North Sea oil, then many companies would be left out on a limb. Now was the time to maintain our growth, reach a good economic level, and bide our time. But Reg wouldn't have it.

He blamed my ego, my unwillingness to allow strangers into the business we had built up ourselves. He blamed my failure to see beyond the specific product I was dealing with, to see it in future business terms. He blamed my stubbornness, my lack of imagination. I scoffed and blamed his greed.

We were both wrong about each other, of course, and secretly we both knew it, but you need words to sling in arguments, and words so often exaggerate.

It all come to a head when I discovered he had already begun undercover negotiations with a hard plastics company. 'Just sounding them out', he had told me when I confronted him with my discovery (I had taken a call when Reg had been out from a director of the other company who was unaware of my resistance to my partner's plans), but I wouldn't be pacified. I had a suspicion of business 'practices' even though I had a genuine respect for Reg's flair, and now I began to be afraid that things were running too fast for me, that my technical skill was no match for business politics. Anger, spurred on by this fear, poured from me.

Reg had had enough: so far as he was concerned he was acting in the company's best interests, negotiating for our growth, afraid that if we didn't expand into other areas we would eventually be swallowed up by the bigger firms. It didn't worry him that we would lose much of our independence: there was no standing still in business for him, only progression or regression. And here I was holding him back, content to let the company slide into mediocrity.

He threw the telephone at me and stormed from our office.

It caught me on the shoulder and I fell back into my chair, stunned not by the blow, but by his irrational behaviour. It took a few seconds for my temper to flare again, then I tore after him.

I was just in time to see his car roar off into the main road. I yanked open the door of my own car, fumbling angrily for my keys as I did so, and jumped in. I gunned the engine as an expression of my rage and swept from the factory yard after him.

The red tail-lights from Reg's car were two tiny points far ahead and I pushed down hard on the accelerator to make them grow larger. We sped through Edenbridge, down the long stretch of straight road that followed, and round the curving bend at the end, then on into the unlit country darkness. I flashed my lights at him, commanding him to stop, wanting to get my hands on him there and then. His car pulled into a side road which would take him across country to Southborough, where he lived, and I slowed just enough to allow me to take the turn.

I jammed on my brakes when I saw he had stopped and was waiting. My car rocked to a halt and I saw him climb from his car and stride back towards me. As he drew near, his hand

184

stretched forward, he began to say. 'Look, we're acting like a couple of ki . . . ' But I ignored the look of apology on his face, his outstretched hand which was ready to take mine in a gesture of appeasement, his words that were meant to bring us both to our senses.

I threw open my door, striking his extended hand, and leapt out, hitting him squarely on the jaw all in one motion. Then I jumped back into the car, snapped it into reverse, and raced backwards into the main road again. I looked forward just in time to see him raise himself on to one elbow, his face lit up in the glare of my headlights. I saw his lips move as though calling my name, and a look of horror sweep across his features.

Then I was in the main road and engulfed in a blinding white light. I felt the car heave and heard someone screaming and through the searing pain that followed I realised I was listening to myself. And then the pain and the light and the screaming became too much and I was dead.

I was floating away, and my car was a mangled wreck, and the cab of the truck that had hit it was buckled and smashed and the driver was climbing from it, his face white and disbelieving, and Reg was crying, trying to pull me from the wreck, calling my name, and refusing to admit what my crumpled body swore to.

And then there was a blankness; and then I was reluctantly pushing myself from my new mother's womb.

I staggered to my feet, all four of them. My head was dazed and spinning, not just with the physical blow it had received, but with the facts that had been revealed to me.

Reg was not the evil man of my dreams: he had been a friend in life and a friend in death. He'd succumbed to my wishes, kept the company small; the extension was a sign that the company was still profitable and growing in the way I had wanted, for it meant no drastic development had taken place, only improvement to existing production. Had he kept it this way out of respect for me, or had his business venture merely fallen through without my added strength? There was no question in my mind;

I *knew* the former was the case. And Reg, the lifelong bachelor, the man I had teased so often about his unmarried status, the friend who had admitted quite openingly there had only ever been one girl for him and I had married her, had finally taken that plunge. Not just for me, a noble act in taking care of my bereaved family, but because he had always loved Carol. He'd known her long before I had (it was he who had introduced us) and our rivalry for her had been fierce until I had won, and then he had become a close friend to both of us.

Our business partnership had often been stormy, but our friendship had rarely rocked. Not until our final conflict, that is. And that was a conflict I know he regretted bitterly. As I now did.

I looked back at the car, its engine dead but the lights still blazing. Disturbed dust swirled and eddied in their beams. Blinking my eyes against the brightness, I staggered forward, out of their glare and into the surrounding darkness. My eyes quickly became used to the sudden change in light and I saw Reg's body slumped half out of the smashed windscreen across the car bonnet. He looked lifeless.

With a gasp of fear, I ran forward and jumped up at the bonnet. One of his arms dangled down the side of the car and his face, white in the moonlight, was turned towards me. I stretched forward and licked the blood from his gashed cheek and ear, begging forgiveness for what I had done, for what I had thought. Don't be dead, I prayed. Don't die uselessly as I had.

He stirred, groaned. His eyes opened and looked directly into mine. And for a moment I swear he recognised me.

His eyes widened and a softness came into them. It was as if he could read my thoughts, as if he understood what I was trying to tell him. Maybe it was only my imagination, maybe he was just in shock, but I'm sure he smiled at me and tried to stroke me with his dangling hand. His eyes suddenly lost their sharpness as consciousness slipped from him. There was little blood on him apart from the gash in his cheek and ear caused by my teeth in our struggle inside the car; my body had broken the glass of the windscreen, he had merely followed through. The steering wheel had prevented him going further and I checked

186

to see it had done no serious damage to his body. It was of the collapsible kind and so he would have a massive bruise across his stomach the next day, but probably nothing more serious. His head must have struck the top of the windscreen frame as he'd gone through and this had caused his blackout. There was no smell of death on him.

Voices came from further down the lane as people left their houses to investigate the sound of the crash. I decided it was time for me to leave; there was nothing here for me any more.

I stretched forward and kissed Reg on his exposed cheek. He stirred but did not regain consciousness.

Then I dropped to all fours and padded away into the night.

Twenty-One

So there you have it, old man. That's it.

Do you believe me?

Or do you think your pain is driving you mad?

Dawn is creeping up on us now, and death – for you – is creeping with it. I knew when I found you here by the roadside last night it was too late to find help for you; the cancer in your stomach had already made its claim.

How long have you walked the roads, caring for no one and no one caring for you? What did life do to make you flee from it? Well, it's over for you now; your years of wandering are done.

I wonder if you do understand all I've told you? I think your closeness to death had made our communication possible. You're in that transitive state which helps the dying receptive to many things they've closed their minds to before. Do you still think there's only blackness waiting for you? Or hell? Heaven? If only it were that simple.

There's not much more to tell you now. I waited, hidden in the darkness, until they had pulled Reg from the car and saw he had regained consciousness again. He actually walked himself to the ambulance which had arrived by then, and I could see him twisting his head, peering into the gloom, looking for me. The people helping him must have thought he was concussed when he kept asking about the dog he'd seen.

I left the area shortly after, paying one last visit to my own grave before going. I don't quite know why I went there; perhaps in some strange way it was to pay my last respects to myself. It was the end of something for me. The end of a life, possibly.

Fresh flowers had been placed at the graveside, and I knew I had not been forgotten. The memory of the husband, the father, the friend, would dull with time, but I'd always be somewhere in a corner of their minds.

For me, it was to be different. The memories might still linger, to surface occasionally, but the emotions had changed. My emotions were fast becoming those of a dog, as though, now my search was over, a ghost had been vanquished. The ghost was my humanness. I felt free, free as any bird in the sky. Free to live as a dog. I ran for nearly a day and, when I finally dropped, the last remnants of my old self had been purged.

That all happened at least – in your terms – two years ago. Memories and old habits still visit me from time to time and I remember myself as a man. But now they only return to me in dreams. Finding you last night, tucked away in this hedge by the roadside, dying and afraid of death, stirred those hidden feelings again. Your dying, the aura that's now around you, drew those feelings out, and with the feelings came the old memories, so clear, so sharp. Perhaps you've helped me too, old man; it would never do for me to relinquish my heritage completely. What was it the badger had said? 'You're special.' Maybe he was right. Maybe everything he told me was right. Maybe I'm meant to remember. Maybe I'm here to help those like you. Maybe.

All I know is that I forget more and more what I was and become what I am.

And by and large, I enjoy what I am. I see life now from a different level: knee-level. It's surprising the difference it makes. It's like always approaching a place from the same direction, then suddenly coming from the opposite way: the familiar changes shape, looks different somehow. It's still the same, but has taken on a new perspective. Know what I mean?

I've travelled the country, swum in the sea. Nobody's ever owned me again, but many have fed me. I've talked with, ate with, and played with so many different species my head aches trying to remember them all. I've been amazed at and chuckled over the neuroses in the animal world: I've met a pig who thought he was a horse; a cow who stuttered; a bull who was bullied by a shrew he shared a field with; a duckling who thought he was ugly (and he was); a goat who thought he was Jesus; a wood-pigeon who was afraid of flying (he preferred to walk everywhere); a toad who could croak Shakespeare sonnets (and little else); an adder who kept trying to stand up; a fox who was vegetarian; and a grouse who never stopped.

I've fought a stoat (we both broke off and ran at the same time – otherwise we'd have both been slaughtered), killed an attacking owl, battled with a rat-pack, and been chased by a swarm of bees. I've teased sheep and irritated horses; I've philosophised with a donkey on existentialism's possible influence on art, ethics and psychology. I've sung with birds and joked with hedgehogs.

And I've made love to seven different bitches.

Time's running out for you now; death's nearly here. I hope what I've told you has helped, I hope it's made some sense to your feverish brain. Can you smell that heavy sweetness in the air; it means I've got to go. It's a lady friend, you see. She lives on a farm three fields away and she's ready for me now. It's just a matter of getting her out of that shed, away from the jealous old farmer; but that shouldn't be too difficult for a smart dog like me.

One other thing before I go: I met Rumbo again the other day. I'd been sleeping under a tree when an acorn hit me on the nose; when I looked around I heard a voice call out 'Hello, squirt,' and there he was above me, grinning all over his little squirrel face. He showered me with a few more acorns, but when I called his name he looked blank, then scurried off. I knew it was him because the voice – thought pattern if you like – was the same; and who else would call me 'squirt'?

It made me feel good, although I had no desire to follow him. It was just good to know someone like Rumbo was around again.

Excuse me now, my lady friend's scent is really becoming too much to ignore. You don't need me anymore anyway, the next part you have to do on your own. At least, I hope I've helped. Maybe we'll bump into each other again sometime.

Good-bye.

Hope you're a dog!

The tramp tried to follow the dog with his tired old eyes as it scampered away, through the broken hedge, into the fields beyond. But the effort was too much.

His body twisted with the pain and seemed to shrivel within the rags he wore as clothes. He lay on his side, his grizzled cheek resting against the damp grass. A solitary ant, not three inches from his eye, gazed at him without expression.

The tramp's lips tried to smile but the pain would not allow it. With his last remaining strength he brought a shaking hand up, and with all the concentration he could summon he placed a finger carefully over the creature's tiny body, but the ant scurried away and hid in the forest of grass. With one last painful shudder, the old man's breath left him and took his life with it.

He died. And waited.

NEL BESTSELLERS

T51277	'THE NUMBER OF THE BEAST'	*Robert Heinlein*	£2.25
T50777	STRANGER IN A STRANGE LAND	*Robert Heinlein*	£1.75
T51382	FAIR WARNING	*Simpson & Burger*	£1.75
T52478	CAPTAIN BLOOD	*Michael Blodgett*	£1.75
T50246	THE TOP OF THE HILL	*Irwin Shaw*	£1.95
T49620	RICH MAN, POOR MAN	*Irwin Shaw*	£1.60
T51609	MAYDAY	*Thomas H. Block*	£1.75
T54071	MATCHING PAIR	*George G. Gilman*	£1.50
T45773	CLAIRE RAYNER'S LIFEGUIDE		£2.50
T53709	PUBLIC MURDERS	*Bill Granger*	£1.75
T53679	THE PREGNANT WOMAN'S BEAUTY BOOK	*Gloria Natale*	£1.25
T49817	MEMORIES OF ANOTHER DAY	*Harold Robbins*	£1.95
T50807	79 PARK AVENUE	*Harold Robbins*	£1.75
T50149	THE INHERITORS	*Harold Robbins*	£1.75
T53231	THE DARK	*James Herbert*	£1.50
T43245	THE FOG	*James Herbert*	£1.50
T53296	THE RATS	*James Herbert*	£1.50
T45528	THE STAND	*Stephen King*	£1.75
T50874	CARRIE	*Stephen King*	£1.50
T51722	DUNE	*Frank Herbert*	£1.75
T52575	THE MIXED BLESSING	*Helen Van Slyke*	£1.75
T38602	THE APOCALYPSE	*Jeffrey Konvitz*	95p

NEL P.O. BOX 11, FALMOUTH TR10 9EN, CORNWALL

Postage Charge:

U.K. Customers 45p for the first book plus 20p for the second book and 14p for each additional book ordered to a maximum charge of £1.63.

B.F.P.O. & EIRE Customers 45p for the first book plus 20p for the second book and 14p for the next 7 books; thereafter 8p per book.

Overseas Customers 75p for the first book and 21p per copy for each additional book.

Please send cheque or postal order (no currency).

Name ....

Address ....

....

Title ....

While every effort is made to keep prices steady, it is sometimes necessary to increase prices at short notice. New English Library reserve the right to show on covers and charge new retail prices which may differ from those advertised in the text or elsewhere.(7)